ANGELA YURIKO SMITH

Bitter Suites

AUTHORTUNITIES

First published by Authortunities Press 2018

100% Human Created

First edition

ISBN: 979-8-90228-926-5

Cover art by Kyra Starr
Editing by Mellissa French

This book was professionally typeset on Reedsy.
Find out more at reedsy.com

Contents

Acknowledgment

Thank you to all the "Halloween People" all over the world that support and love this story. Thank you to my family who love and support me even though I am an incurable "Halloween People."

A 2018 Bram Stoker Awards® Finalist for Superior Achievement in Long Fiction

Find out more about the Horror Writers Association, a nonprofit organization of writers and publishing professionals around the world, dedicated to promoting dark literature and the interests of those who write it.

Find out more information at horror.org.

Cherry Pop

It was my 18th birthday, and I was finally going to die in a safe, monitored environment. My mom freaked out, of course. They didn't have stuff like this when she was going through the angst. She couldn't understand how important it was to me. All my friends had already died once or twice. The school counselors even said it was developmentally necessary, the earlier the better. And now here I was, ever the late bloomer—*thanks Mom*—finally getting my first turn.

I knew The Bitter Suites would have everything I needed, so I rushed over after work with only my PaID credit and a cherry soda. The soda was to drink in celebration after my death cherry was popped. I thought that was pretty funny. Apparently I have a crappy sense of humor because no one else laughed about it. That's one reason why I have so much angst. No one understands me.

My mom and I argued for months but she knew once I hit the big one-eight she would lose legal jurisdiction over me and I'd be free to make my own decisions. My first, as a new adult, would be to relieve some of my blues.

"First time?" asked the girl behind the counter. I nodded. She smiled in a distant way that clearly communicated *I get paid to be interested*. Didn't matter to me if she was interested or not. I was just here to get on with my life.

"Do you have any preferred method of death?" she asked. I had thought about it all a lot, but I could never decide. They all sounded equally dramatic and satisfying.

"I was wondering if there was some kind of combination package," I said. "Maybe I can kind of start with poison, wrist cutting and then maybe hanging? And I've thought a lot about drowning too." She raised her eyebrows at me, clearly annoyed. "I can't decide, they all sound perfect." I shrugged and smiled.

"You can only have one death per stay but I *can* arrange for a variety of methods to be available to you as a blended death." She shuffled through some papers on the desk and pulled out a glossy brochure. I leaned over the counter as she explained.

I was surprised at how many ways to die there were. There were the solo experiences, like I was choosing, and romantic couple deaths. There was an *In Childbirth* experience for new moms to help bond with their babies, an *Old Yeller* package for canine enthusiasts to bring their pets and the whole *Egyptian Mummified Alive!* package that had caught my eye in the first place. In the end I decided to have my first death plain so I could experience it the way it was meant to be. A *Romeo and Juliet Valentine Death* looked awesome though. I pointed at it.

"I'll be back with my girlfriend to try that one out," I told her. She just nodded and went on with her spiel. In the end, I paid a little more to have up to four near-deaths available to me. I would start out with poison. When that kicked in I'd slice my wrists open, flaying them lengthwise and not cross wise, as she instructed.

When I had a good bleed going, I'd hang myself but the rope would break just short of snapping my neck so I could fall into a bathtub of water. A toaster would be set up to fall in after me so I could be electrocuted.

"That's a pretty big first death," she told me, friendlier now. "But it is your birthday. I'll throw in the finishing toaster no charge." I grinned. I've heard one of the biggest benefits to recreational suicide was the lack of fear afterwards. The attendant was older than me by a few years, but cute. Maybe I'd be fearless enough to ask her out afterwards.

After I'd signed my legals and swiped my PaID, she gave me my suite number, keycard and a folded pile of terry cloth. I fumbled with the pile and dropped the keycard. The rest of what she gave me hit the ground when I bent over to retrieve the card. Trying to look less awkward, and failing, I picked up a bathrobe from the mess at my feet and held it out to her, eyebrows raised.

"It doesn't look like you brought a change of clothes," she said. "This is a courtesy robe provided by The Bitter Suites to help make your stay more enjoyable. Death can be messy, but your clothes don't have to be." She smiled brightly.

"Do they ever fail to bring someone back?" I asked. I could feel the whisper of a tremble begin deep in my bowels. She looked at me for a long minute. It was long enough for me to take note of the cornflower blue of her eyes and how her long lashes began as black but faded to a honey blonde at the tips. She wasn't cute at all, I decided. She was stunning. My heart did a crazy spin.

"Yes, technically the Resuscitators could fail," she answered finally. "But if it was a fail-safe guaranteed bring-back, wouldn't that make it less exciting?" She batted her eyelashes at me then, like a cartoon femme fatale, I swear. "And here, we're all about being exciting."

Another tremor had started up inside me but it had nothing to do with experiencing my first recreational suicide. By that point, I think I'd forgotten everything but the lovely angel that was now escorting me to my destination, pressing the keycard firmly into my palm. As she guided me backwards into an elevator, she piled my towels and robe back into my arms.

"Have a fun death," she said grinning, "See you on the other side." I leaned against the back wall as the doors closed, and realized I was in full crush. My face flushed, my heart raced like a scared cat, and suddenly I could care less about my impending suicide. The entire point of dying was to appreciate being alive. As I thought of the girl I just left downstairs, I realized all I wanted to do was get this over with so I could ask her out.

The elevator doors slid open and I stepped into the hallway, clutching my towels. Signs on the wall directed me to go right to find my room number. The hall was wide and bright. Thick carpet, visually screaming with garish geometric designs in orange and red, muffled my footfalls.

The loud carpet contrasted with the lack of color or design anywhere else. The walls were white and without texture. The doors, also white, were inset along both sides at regular intervals. Plastic squares were stuck to each door at eye level, displaying the room number. I followed along, reading door numbers to find my own. A shriek came through one door as I passed, startling me. It was a woman's voice followed by panicked sobs.

"No...no, please! I've changed my mind!" There was a muffled crash and a thump. I heard running footsteps and then another thump. She cried out, her voice was rising in pitch again. "Please, I don't want to die! No!" She shrieked again, but her voice was cut off mid-scream. There was another solid thump and I tried to imagine what death she had chosen. I hoped I didn't chicken out like that.

I listened at the door, feeling like a perv, but I couldn't leave yet. The silence was liquid, stopping my ears with quiet. My heart pounded an alert... *eavesdropper...eavesdropper...eavesdropper!* My own body was intent on giving me up. After a full minute, a deep sigh came from inside the room, and then a voice.

"Okay, that should do it. Let's bring her back." A second voice crackled over a radio.

"Okay, coming in." A door opened and multiple feet trampled the room to the sounds of beeping equipment and clattering metal. Something glass shattered, followed by a gush of profanity.

"Dammit! I have to pay for that! Who put it on the edge?" Angry exclamations followed, too low to discern enunciation. Other voices laughed. "Don't worry about it, just say she did it. She'll never know." There was murmured assent from the rest of the room.

"Okay, ladies and gentlemen, let's bring back the star of our show. Stick her now!" The room settled into silence until someone began a quiet countdown... *3...2...1...and...* a ragged breath ruined the hush, followed by spasmodic coughing.

"And here she is!" There was applause and whistles. "Welcome back to life!" The choking had subsided, and the woman that was just begging started thanking everyone in a sniveling whine. "Thank you everyone, I'm so glad to be alive!" She started crying loudly. "Eve...everything is so beautiful!"

I rolled my eyes. My own death was waiting. I looked at my keycard again. Room 33. The door I'd been listening in at was 24. My destiny waited just a few doors down. I started down the hall. As I moved closer to the death I'd reserved, I started to feel a little reserved.

My mom had advised me against trying a suicide trip. She said it was a dangerous fad, and you could get addicted. I had told her I was just going to try a near death experience when I turned 21... not go the whole way. She didn't believe me, said a near death would just be a gateway death that would make me crave more. As I stopped in front of my room I wondered if she was right. Would I get addicted?

The square, plastic card on the door claimed to be 33. My keycard was stuck to my sweaty palm, and my hand was slightly shaking as I slid it. The door chimed and opened. The automated lights went on, and I knew my time had started. I now had an hour to kill.

Pushing the door open, I expected it to creak eerily like an old horror movie, but no sound came from the well maintained hinges. The Bitter Suites was no dive hotel and had great reviews. I pondered postponing this suicide trip to request squeaking hinges. The room was non-refundable, but my first time needed to be perfect—and I realized I was just stalling. *Man up*, I told myself. I went into the room and closed the door behind me.

I'm not sure what I expected, but this wasn't it. The hotel room looked disappointingly ordinary. There was a bed with a practical looking bedspread in an orange and red pattern to compliment the hall carpet. Fortunately, the carpet in this room was a little more tame.

There was a television, a microwave and a coffee pot on a counter near the door. On the opposite end of the room was a large mirror and another door. I expected that's where the Resuscitation Crew was waiting. The thought made me feel more relaxed, and I looked around for how to get this party started. On the counter, in front of the microwave, I noticed a small bottle with a tag.

I went over and picked it up. Made of black plastic, there was a skull and crossbones symbol printed on it in toxic green. I turned over the tag. It read *Drink me*. My reflection caught my gaze as I stood there.

I looked awkward in my own skin. It hung too tight where it should be loose and too loose where it should be tight. Hair and shiny pores were all over the place. I don't like who I am. I don't know how to be cool with people and always say the wrong thing. I suspect the few friends I have probably laugh at me when I'm not around. It's painful being me. I pointed at myself in the mirror and leaned forward.

"That's why I'm going to kill you," I said to my reflection. "I'm tired of you. This is going to grow you up." I popped the little bottle's top and swallowed the contents.

I sat down on the bed to wait. I'd never experienced poison before, nor any kind of death, so I wasn't sure what to expect. I tried to look casual, but I wasn't sure what I should be doing while I waited. I tried not to look at the large mirror where I was sure a crew was watching. I picked at the bedspread, tracing my finger along one of the geometric lines. *Hmmmm....* I said out loud and I checked the time on my phone. Two minutes, and I still felt nothing. I stood up and faced the mirror.

"I'm not sure the poison is working…" I said. Suddenly, pain knifed through my innards. I bent over double, shocked. My insides felt like they were flayed open and bile crept up the back of my throat. The back of my eyeballs pricked with heat and felt like they were swelling. "Never mind…" I gasped. I fell to my knees and barfed everywhere.

There was no more quiver of anticipation in the pit of my stomach now. I was being twisted from the inside. Vicious, invisible torque was turning me into a corkscrew. Cold sweat zipped up my spine to lodge at the base of my skull where white stars danced against my vision. I was going to die. I barfed again. Someone had entered the room.

"Hey, I've been assigned to assist you if you need it. Do you need help?" I reached out a trembling hand, and let it rest on the boot in front of me.

"Poison… not good," I gasped. "It hurts…" He laughed.

"No pain, no gain." He crouched down and put an arm around me. "You are taking your time and we want to make sure you get a full value experience, so I'm going to assist you. Time for the wrists." He laid a straight razor on the carpet in front of me. The blade was in a cardboard sleeve marked *For your hygiene.* "Here you go. You picked a full plate for your first time."

By now I was crouched on the carpet in a fetal position. The pain in my gut was phenomenal. My lips were dry and my tongue overly wet. My own drool made me want to vomit again. I couldn't swallow, so I let it run down my chin.

"Make it stop," I gurgled. Mom was right. This was too much pain. I should have never done this. The big man rubbed my back and made soothing noises. He picked up the razor and removed the cardboard sleeve from the blade. He grabbed my hand and turned it over, pulling it out. "Let me help you, kid," he said. "You don't have much time." My vision cleared enough to see the razor at my skin and I tried to pull away but my muscles felt like rotting seaweed. I was weak.

The blade slid into the soft flesh of my wrist far too easily, lengthwise and not cross wise, as instructed. Time hiccupped to a stop and I thought maybe it hadn't cut me after all… and then blood began to bubble out. He let go of my wrist and I pulled my bleeding limb to my chest to cradle it. It didn't hurt compared to the pain in the rest of my body. The drool from my face was mixing with the blood pooling around my knees, but my insides hurt too much to care. I vomited again, adding more nasty to the mix.

"Okay, we gotta get this kid strung up. He's going faster than he should," The man called loudly. He leaned back over me. "Did you come here on an empty stomach? You were supposed to eat first!"

"I wanted… money's worth…" I gasped. I was crying now. My face was wet with tears, blood, spit and puke and I wasn't sure which was the worst. All options were humiliating at this point. I hadn't realized death was so disgusting.

There were more people in the room now and I was being dragged to the bathroom. My vision was a haze and all I could see were shadowy impressions. At random intervals my sight would clear and I'd have a surreal image snapped into my brain before it all dimmed again. Feet, faces, a door handle… and then a rope hanging from a large hook in the ceiling. I remembered I chose hanging.

"No…." I was full on pathetic, I know. I tried to struggle. I just wanted to lay on the floor, curled up like a snail and die. The pain was too much. Puking hurt, not puking hurt... everything hurt. They started stretching me out and lifting me up as a team. I tried to kick at them, but my legs were useless. I heard splashing and someone cussed.

"Watch the toaster! I don't want a freebie!" The rope slid across my face, smearing the muck. I was going to throw up again, held upright like this. I started dry heaving. "He's going to hurl again...! Drop him—drop him!" I felt the hands let go and I was swinging free.

The pressure on my neck wasn't sudden as I had imagined. The hands let go in pairs, not at once. The effect was a gradual, reluctant choking. The bile came rushing up only to find itself at an impasse. Some escaped, burning the inside of my nose as it forced its way free. The rest stayed trapped in my throat, choking me along with the tightening rope. My vision was going... I was going... and the pain ebbed to the back of my mind as I prepared to let it all go. From far away, someone yelled *Drop him now!* And the pressure around my neck was gone.

I fell free, splashing into cool water. My limbs flailed on their own accord, gravity their new master. I felt the water close over my head and I sank. I tried to suck in a breath but water filled my lungs. I saw the inside of the bathtub where I was now submerged with vivid detail—a pubic hair, bubbles sticking to the inside of the fiberglass, a tiny pink fiber. I tensed my muscles to flail, to fight my way to air, and then a flash burned burned everything... pain...regret...suffering... and I floated away in relief.

Life came back with no foreplay. Breath was the first thought I remember having. It filled up the vacuum that had developed in my chest with violence. I took in too much and my beleaguered lungs rebelled and expelled it back. I coughed spasmodically.

"Welcome back!" said someone. I recognized it as the voice that had helped me before. Gratitude overcame me and I became aware that I was sobbing. I didn't care. The room applauded me and I continued to cry. The joy at being alive eclipsed all other pain. My throbbing wrist was a mute symphony, my pulse keeping time. I was drenched, stank of vomit and was sore all over but I was *alive*... and that became the singularly most important fact. Nothing else mattered.

They lifted me onto the bed, wrapping me in blankets while the Resuscitators worked on pasting me back together. I became warm, but the heat was radiating from the love in my heart. It beat still and I was aware at how precious that percussion really was. One day, it would cease. I would cease. Medical technology wasn't yet able to keep us going indefinitely so all I had at this moment was… this moment… and it was so, absolutely sweet. I vowed to cherish every precious moment I had left. I lay back and let the resuscitation crew work their magic.

A few hours later I was back on my feet and dragging through the lobby, sore and exhausted but exuberant with living. My clothes were as trashed as I felt, but there was no resuscitation crew for them. I had forgotten to change into my courtesy robe, and there was little the crew could do to clean off the vomit and blood stains. I'd be a triumphant mess on the train home and proud of it.

I had my soda ready and I carried it to the counter to see if there was an opener… and an opening in her social schedule. She was waiting on a client so I leaned against the counter, pointedly, to wait.

The customer looked like the dramatic type, dressed completely in Gothic black attire. Her hair was teased up vintage 80s style and as dark as her clothes. Heavy, Egyptian looking eye liner and a large silver ankh completed her look. She had probably spent hours getting her look right for this. She glanced at me as I studied her and smiled with genuine warmth. I liked her.

"First time?" I asked her. The two girls looked at each other and giggled. I felt awkward, like I was the butt of their joke. "Can just you open this," I said, to change the subject. I handed my bottle to the honey dipped angel behind the counter. The Gothic girl put a hand on my shoulder.

"I'm not laughing at you," she said the girl in black. She looked into my eyes and I couldn't help smiling back. "It's just that I'm here all the time. I practically work here." That made me feel better. The counter girl handed me back my drink, opened.

"It was a twist top," she said. I swear she rolled her eyes at me. I decided not to ask her out after all. The other girl leaned over and read my bottle's label.

"Cherry pop to celebrate a first time with death," she said. "Appropriate."

I flushed and felt very macho. I had died, come back, and it was awesome. I was a survivor. I was a warrior. I tipped my bottle to the ladies in what I hoped seemed a gallant gesture, took a deep swig, and turned to go.

"And it won't be my last," I said, pushing the door open with my back, looking directly at the counter girl.

"If you enjoyed your stay, please leave us a review online," she said.

"Everything is five stars," I said, and I pushed my way outside to enjoy my new lease on life.

Poinsettia Creams

The couple entered the lobby of The Bitter Suites, arms linked close enough they were practically Siamese twins. The receptionist didn't need to look at the reservation book to see that this was her *Romeo & Juliet* couple, paid in full already with a bottle of champagne reserved as a post-resuscitation toast.

They walked all the way to the front desk without even glancing at their surroundings. The girl blushed and bit her lip whenever she felt her companion's eyes upon her. The man pulled her close with a reassuring arm. The receptionist inwardly sighed and resigned herself to an uncomfortably sweet encounter.

"You must be our recently engaged couple here for your romantic date with death," she said. "Stella and John." As expected, the girl giggled and blushed and the young man puffed his chest out while pulling her closer. *If he wraps that arm any tighter,* the receptionist thought, *he may as well just strangle her now and save his money.* Outwardly, she smiled.

"How romantic," she said. "But you didn't opt for the extra roses, wine and chocolate. Was that an oversight?" Predictably, the girl scowled and looked up at him with narrowed eyes. John caught the look and its meaning. His male ego twisted between the two feminine forces working against him and his budget before surrendering.

"I'm so glad you caught that," he said. He looked down at Stella."I meant to ask – I thought you probably didn't want chocolate and wine with your poison. That might not go together too well." John looked hopeful as doubt flitted across her face.

"Oh, in that case you can have your poison delivered either in the chocolate or the wine for just a little extra." The receptionist loved this game of placing dollar amounts on affection with some of the clients. "We have Poinsettia Creams that are to die for." Stella made an excited *oh!* from where she nestled in her man's armpit, and he knew he had lost.

"Just a little extra…? Then of course! Nothing is too good for my princess." The receptionist hid her smug satisfaction behind a smile and busied herself with upgrading their package, adding a decent gratuity. Once the legals and payment were finished she gave them their keycard and sent them on their way.

"Enjoy your stay at The Bitter Suites," she said as she escorted them to the elevator. "You're in room 77 on our Seventh Heaven level. There is a Resuscitation Crew already waiting for you."

"What floor would that be on?" John asked. He peered at the receptionist's name tag. "Azrael…? Pretty name." Stella glared at him. The receptionist hoped they weren't planning on having children.

"That would be the *seventh* floor," she answered as waved them into the elevator. "Have fun lovebirds!" The door slid closed and the receptionist's smile evaporated like rain in the desert. She allowed herself a satisfying eye roll before parking herself back behind her desk to wait for the next client. She hated love for love's sake.

Above her, the couple was just exiting the elevator onto their floor. The carpet was a dizzying display of hearts in all shades of red and pink. The walls were painted to look like they were clouds and golden sun rays with cherubs frolicking in their downy depths. Above, the ceiling was all twilit sky, sunset and galaxies blending into the wall pattern and set in countless silver stars above. The man counted at least five full moons from the elevators to the end of the hall. Inset lighting lined the hall's length creating a luminous effect on the stellar panorama. He whistled.

"This is worth every bit," he said. Stella agreed. She looked up at her future husband, overcome with passion. "I will die for you." He turned to her, his heart overflowing with gratitude that this angel had fallen for the likes of him. "And I'll die for you, as many times as you need," he answered, and he kissed her deeply. "Our time has started," he said, voice husky with heat. "We need to get to our room."

Together, they stumbled down the hallway. He was following the numbered cards on the door while she allowed herself to be led, her gaze mesmerized by the painted spectacle over their heads. He located their door, slid the keycard and led her through.

The room didn't disappoint. It was as if they had stepped into a medieval chamber. The walls were painted to look like rough stone. The flooring was covered in plush carpet with a realistic pattern that simulated slate pavers. Heavy pewter sconces hung from the walls, lit with holographic flames. In the middle of the room was a large, round bed draped in sheer fabrics. The edge of the bed was lined with more of the holographic flames, giving the appearance that it was floating in a bed of fire.

An altar festooned in fresh roses was to one side of the bed. On it was their Dom Pérignon in a pewter bucket of ice, two silver chalices, a silver dagger and a small, pewter plate that held two chocolates decorated with poinsettia flowers piped in frosting. Stella clasped her hands to her heart.

"This is so beautiful," she said. Her eyes welled with tears. She stepped away from John and let her coat and purse dramatically fall to the floor before running to the bed and collapsing upon it. She pulled her shirt open, exposing her delicate collarbones and white neck with one hand while flinging the other across the bed. Her feet draped over the side, licked by artificial flames. "Kill me now," she said, and swooned.

"I can't wait to die with you," said John. "But we did pay extra for the ambiance. We have this place for one, amazing hour. Let's try out that bed out for something besides death..." Stella sat straight up and glared at him.

"Not with the Resuscitators watching!" she said in a low voice. Her eyes scanned the room until they found a large mirror held in an ornate frame at the back of the room. "They are back there right now, talking about us. Can't you just be romantic for once?" John felt like all he did was be romantic with

Stella and it was always expensive. That would all change once they were married, he knew. He just had to keep up with her until then.

"Sorry," he said. "It's just that you are so beautiful. You look just like Juliet from the old movies, and I am your Romeo." He picked up the plate with the chocolates and knelt before her on one knee. "Juliet, Juliet... let down your golden hair." She giggled.

"Stop it! That's not even in the movie." He picked one of the chocolates up from the plate and wondered how much it cost before he held it up to her lips.

"Die for me, my sweet darling. Let this sweet death bring us closer together." His eyes fixed on hers as he touched the chocolate to her lips. Obediently, she bit into it.

"Erm, that's actually really good," she said around the bite. He popped the rest of the chocolate into her mouth and she finished it. "John, do you promise to marry me and always take care of me like your princess?" He nodded. "Then I eat this chocolate to prove my undying love to you by actually dying."

"Now me," he said. He held the chocolate up to his own lips, but she put her hand over it, preventing him from eating. "First tell me why you love me."

"Honey, we have to eat them at the same time," he said. "Let me eat this and then I'll tell you." He tried to push her hand away but instead she slapped the chocolate from his hand. It landed on the carpet. "First, tell me why you love me." John looked for his candy, saw where it had rolled and then looked back at Stella. He knew if he didn't just cater to her demand they were going no further with this.

"Stella, my beautiful girl," he said, looking intensely into her eyes. "I love you because you are the prettiest woman I know. The most beautiful in the whole city. Maybe even the world. Most likely the universe." Stella wrinkled her nose at him and giggled.

He kissed her then and pressed her back onto the bed feeling his passion rise. He could still taste the candy on her tongue. It made his lips feel numb. She responded with equal heat at first but then pushed him back.

"I don't feel good," she said. Her flawless skin was beaded in little pearls of sweat. She swallowed convulsively as her eyes teared up. Her skin flushed.

"It's the poison starting to work," he said. "When do you want me to stab you?" She scooted to the edge of the bed and wrapped her arms around her middle. "Don't talk to me right now..." A loud belch rolled out of her followed by a surprised whimper and she clamped a hand over her mouth. "Where's the bathroom?" she asked from behind her palm. He sat up and started to slide his arms around her.

"Don't touch me!" She slapped his hands away and fell to her knees at the side of the bed. "Bathroom!" She belched involuntarily and started gagging. John sat back, insulted. "You wanted this," he said. "The bathroom is over here." He started helping her up but she pulled away from him, curling at his feet. An animal cry came from her that choked out abruptly as she began heaving.

He tried to push her away as she retched onto his feet, a bubbling noise his only warning. The sudden gush of wet heat soaking his shoes shocked him, and he kicked out instinctively. His foot caught her square in the face, knocking her back as she vomited chocolate and the remains of their romantic lunch a few hours ago. Strands of her hair were stuck against her damp skin and a trail of blood began an exodus out of her left nostril. She sprawled on her back, arms and legs waving like an overturned roach before she rolled back over and continued heaving.

"Hold ... my hair," she said between gags. Recoiling, John sat back on the bed, overcome with disgust. Stella could be difficult and self-centered at the best of times, but her looks made up for her sour nature. His princess had transformed into a harpy, hunched over a pool of vomit and blood. John hoped clean up was included in the price.

"I'm not feeling this anymore," he said. He kicked off his shoes and started peeling off his sock.

"You kicked me... in the fash!" Her words were slurred but she seemed to have expelled all the contents of her stomach for the moment. She knelt in the mess, muck covered hands held out in front of her and tears starting to leak from her eyes. "It's not supposed to be like this. You ordered the wrong death. My clothes are ruined." She glared at him lopsidedly. Her dilated pupils were mismatched, giving her a cross eyed appearance. "And you kicked me."

"I'm sorry, Stella darling. It was an accident." John didn't really want to hold and comfort the mess in front of him, but he held out his arms dutifully. John's father had warned him against Stella. He told John to avoid a high maintenance woman unless he won the lottery. *A woman you gotta work too hard for ain't worth it,* his dad had said. John had to admit to himself, Stella was definitely a lot of work.

"You always have… ta be a… a jerk!" Stella struggled to her feet. "I hate you… and maybe I won… I won marry you anymore." This wasn't the first time Stella had threatened to break off the marriage and usually it sent John into a panic. All she had to do was pout a little and he was jelly in her hands. It was hard work, but he always seemed to be able to make things right with her.

Her usually perfect makeup ran with the tears under her eyes, hair flat and dirty with tendrils stuck to her sweaty neck. Her nose still dribbled blood that smeared with saliva across her cheek. He could smell the acidic odor of vomit on her from where he sat. His stomach turned and he dropped his arms, taking back his offer of embrace. She stumbled forward and stepped on something. Trying to turn her foot over to see, Stella wobbled and collapsed on the carpet where she rolled about, trying to see what was on her foot. John's Poinsettia Cream was smashed between her toes.

"Why haven… you eaten your choco yet?" He had never noticed how her voice increased in pitch to a whine before and it raked across his nerves like steel wool on a sunburn.

"Stella, I'm not eating it *now*. It's stuck to your foot. I have to rinse my work shoes before they stink." He stood, avoiding eye contact. He remembered the Resuscitation Crew that was watching and wondered if they were laughing at him.

"No! I ate the chocoyet. You have…eat… your chocamet." Stella picked the candy off her toe and threw it at John. Her throw was weak and it fell at his feet. The poison was working through her system and she burped. "Eat you chalkenet!"

"You *had* to have the expensive chocolate poison. And now look at my shoes!" John held one shoe up to her, pinching the heel between his index and thumb to avoid the gore. "You puked on me! This isn't romantic. You look terrible. I'm not doing this." John kicked the smashed chocolate back towards her. "You have both." He started to the bathroom.

"No! No!..." Stella scrambled crookedly to the small table and grabbed the silver dagger, knocking everything else down. "Ima kill...you!" She staggered towards John who turned just in time to see her stumbling at him, wildly swinging the blade. He twisted to one side and she missed sticking the dagger into his chest. Instead, it sliced through the soft part of his upper arm. He cried out and shoved her back. Stella's foot caught in the bed linens and she fell.

"You...hip me!" Her eyes bulged at him, unfocused and angry.

"You tried to stab me," he said, backing up. She crawled toward him, tried to get up using the blade as a support. It twisted out of her weakened grip, cutting her palm. She collapsed and stared numbly at the blood on her hand and then up at John. Her bloodshot eyes lit up with the toxic cocktail of adrenaline and malice.

"Ow." Her lips barely moved as she spoke, her low voice forcing its way past her clenched teeth. "We are supposed... to die... together." She hoisted herself to her feet. To John, she looked like a witch from a nightmare. Blood, vomit and blade approached him. He glanced behind him, looking for escape. He saw the mirror.

"Can I get some help?" he said to the room. "This is going too far..." There was no response from the mirror.

"This was... my dream...and you ruin... it..." She tripped over her own feet towards him and fell to the carpet again. Scared, John turned and ran into the bathroom. He slammed the door behind him and locked it.

"Help!" he shouted. "I don't really want to die! Not like this!" Stella had dragged herself to the bathroom door. He could hear her nails scrabbling against the wood. She pressed her face against the crack at the bottom, hiccuping. John could smell her rancid breath wafting up.

"You... an jerk," she said from the other side of the door, quieter now. John bent closer to hear what she was saying. "I an too...good...fer you. Hate you...I slept with... you frens..." Stella's breath wheezed from her in a hiss and she was finally silent.

John waited in the bathroom, surprised at his lack of surprise. He leaned his forehead against the door, expecting tears. Instead, a feeling of relief washed through him. After a full minute he quietly unlocked the door and peeked out. She lay against the door jam, still clutching the dagger, not breathing. Across the room another door opened and three figures entered.

"I am so sorry, man," said one. "That was intense. Do you want to be here when she wakes up?" John looked down at the spittle and blood stained creature that lay stinking on the floor and saw her as herself for the first time.

"No, I think I better be gone," he said. "So much for undying love." He retrieved one of his shoes from the bathroom floor.

"Don't blame you. You can get your injuries taken care of at First Aid in the lobby," said the Resuscitator. "Clean your shoes there, too." The other two had laid Stella out and were preparing to revive her. John nodded. He knelt down next to his former fiance, took her hand and slipped the engagement ring off her finger and into his pocket.

"I'll leave her cab fare at the front desk," he said. He picked up the Dom Pérignon from where it lay half under the bed, glowing in the artificial flames, and left the room. He would need a drink after this and he may as well start with the good stuff. He had paid for it.

Downstairs, the receptionist waited at her desk. John suddenly noticed the cornflower blue of her eyes and how her long lashes began as black but faded to a honey blonde at the tips. Her hair was the same, dark roots that faded to soft gold. She helped him to First Aid and even took his shoes to be cleaned while his arm was stitched up. She asked no questions when he left cab fare for his fiance, but smiled comfortingly.

"Did you enjoy the poinsettia creams?" she asked. John just shrugged.

"I didn't get a chance to try them," he said.

"There's always next time," she said, and then she batted her eyelashes at him, like a damsel in distress from an old movie. John turned the ring in his pocket between his fingers and wondered if he was reading too much into that eyelash flutter. Whatever it may or may not have meant, the minute breeze her lashes created was enough to blow Stella from his mind. John felt better than he had in a long time.

"Yeah," he said hesitantly, and then he brightened. "Until next time." He handed her the bottle of champagne and pushed his way out the door, leaving The Bitter Suites, and old flames, behind him.

Tomato Leaf Tea

The old woman shambled halfway across the lobby without the receptionist hearing her. Upon reaching the counter, the old woman leaned forward, squinting at the girl's name tag.

"Azrael," she said. "Can you help me?" The receptionist had noted the woman's approach by now, and had watched her slow, stiff approach. Her hand rested on the name she had just written in the hotel's registry.

"Of course," she said. "You must be my 2 o'clock client, Maeve. We have a nostalgic death waiting for you. Welcome to The Bitter Suites." The old woman blinked, surprised, and then smiled. Her look was soft but the light didn't reach her eyes. They were full of sad shadows. She nodded.

"I have my things prepared, as instructed," she said. She held up a small satchel. "Here's my change of clothes in case I need them and I paid online."

"How set are you on poisoning by tomato leaf tea?" asked Azrael. "Tomato greens aren't really poisonous. That's a myth, so we had to supplement the toxin. Is that okay? It will be a tomato leaf blend." Maeve shook her head.

"If I was after accuracy in death, I wouldn't pay for the nostalgia," she said.

"When I was little, my mother always threatened that she would make me drink tomato leaf tea if I was bad." Azrael raised her eyebrows, questioning, but Maeve said no more.

The afternoon sun shone through the lobby's glass door, causing Maeve's thinning white hair to glow lightly around her lined face. The two women locked gazes, studying each other. The old woman's eyes were pale and washed out, a faded mirror of the receptionist's sky blue. They had nothing in common except gender, but an understanding passed between them.

"You know death won't change the past," said Azrael. "It may not even change how you feel about it."

"But it *may*, and that's all I need," said Maeve. "I'm ready when you are." The receptionist finished the rest of the check-in process with the old woman and walked her to the elevator, placing a keycard into her palm and pushing the buttons for her.

"I hope you find the change you seek," she said, backing out as the elevator doors slid shut, parting the two women.

Down the elevator went, taking Maeve into the basement levels. She exited the elevator on the .03rd floor, beneath the city surface. As she stepped out, she imagined she could feel the vibrations of the city trains in the walls. There were so many people in the world now, she mused, every inch of the earth felt packed, above the surface and below.

She stepped out of the elevator and looked down at her keycard for the first time. Number .022. The sign in front of the elevator directed her to go right, and she quickly found her door. She looked down the hallway, noting the worn, green carpet and vintage wallpaper. It reminded her of her grandmother's dining room, all heavy velvet scrolls and leaves. She wondered if it was an intentional decorating choice or an oversight from the past. A carved wooden chair with gold velvet upholstery sat halfway down the hall, against the wall. *This floor must be for the old people,* she thought. *There's even places to rest as we hobble slowly along our way.*

Maeve wasn't happy about getting old. She wasn't happy about many things that had happened in her life, but she handled age like she had the rest of it – fixed what she could and moved on. She had never tried a recreational death as it was a recently new fad, but she hoped it would bring her peace.

It took her three tries to get the keycard to work. Her hands trembled lightly and her fingers had difficulty maneuvering the card in the reader. When she finally got the key to work, she pushed through as quickly as she could before it locked on her again, dropping her bundle in the process. She groaned as she bent over to retrieve it, not because anything hurt, but by habit.

Maeve walked into the room and set her things on the crocheted popcorn bedspread. The room had the same worn feel as the hallway. A heavily draped window let in the late afternoon light peek around its curtained edges. The furniture, while in good condition, probably had to be purchased from antique shops. It was all from before her time, a fact she might mention in her review afterwards. This wasn't her era, but a few generations before. She walked to the window, curious to see what kind of view waited three floors below ground.

Pulling back the drapes, she was surprised to see the street she had lived on as a girl. She knew it was just a projection from the address she had submitted, but the effect was instant. Her eyes stung as she took in the suburban landscape with its wide, sun baked sidewalks and squat, ugly houses. She had hated how that neighborhood looked. Like the residents, every house conformed to an unspoken, and boring, standard.

When a German lady had moved in, she broke the code by planting a vegetable garden in her front yard, insuring herself as a topic of gossip for the next decade. Even the children, Maeve included, had participated in the whispers. They had all be cruel. She shook her head to clear it of the memories and then chuckled at the irony. Memories are what she had paid extra for.

A chair and a side table sat before the window, turned to face the pretend street of her past. An electric kettle waited with a teacup and saucer. On the saucer were two tea bags, each in a paper envelope. Printed on the paper were the words *Tomato Leaf Tea courtesy of The Bitter Suites.* If only her mother could have seen her now, acting on the long ago threat.

"Bring it on, Mama." She turned the kettle on.

As a girl she'd always taken the threat seriously. Because of it, she'd never liked tea, suspicious that it would be laced with herbal toxins. As an adult she knew her mother hadn't been serious and would have never hurt her only child, not physically anyway. Sometimes the worst damage hides under the skin, bruising the heart.

Maeve never forgave her mother for sending her to live with her grandparents. When Maeve was in her gawky preteens, a new man had come into her mother's life, one who didn't appreciate a mouthy tomboy giving him the stink eye. Her mother had agreed to send Maeve away "for the summer," but when the holidays ended Maeve was registered by her grandmother in a new school.

She had always felt temporary in her grandmother's home so she never bothered making friends. When she graduated, no one had come to congratulate her. Her grandmother was ill, her grandfather had passed away and her mother had simply forgotten. Maeve never called her to ask why, she had just moved on. After the ceremony she walked through the high school parking lot alone as families embraced. She didn't hear from her mother again for years, when her mother was alone and suddenly needed her. Her mother had gone terminal.

Maeve had her own life by then, and there had been no room for her mother. She did her minimum duty as a daughter and arranged for her mother to be transferred to a hospice facility, set up automatic transfer for the fees and continued with her life, intending to visit someday. Her mother passed in less than six months.

Maeve had meant to let her mother stay there alone and unloved as punishment for her own desertion, she realized now, but Maeve had intended to eventually visit. Her procrastination had ruined her last chance to know her mother. The guilt had colored her life since. The electric kettle started whistling, cutting through Maeve's thoughts with a shrill cry.

She hobbled to the kettle, opened a tea bag and dropped it in the cup. The other she put in her pocket. As she poured the hot water she wondered what she was trying to accomplish by playing with death. It didn't really matter now, she'd already paid for this. She would figure it out, or she wouldn't. She took her tea cup and saucer to the chair and sat down.

Her eyes stared at the fabricated suburban scene in front of her, but the street she saw was in her mind, many years ago. She'd hated how the houses looked, but she had friends in that place. There had been at least two children in every house and the lot of them had formed a complicated hierarchy of relationships. She hadn't been the most popular, but she always had the best ideas for adventures and games, ensuring her place at the center of things. She sipped the tea, leaving the tea bag to continue steeping.

The tea was bitter and strong. She flipped over the tea's envelope and read the ingredients. *Contains tomato leaves, aconite, hemlock and belladonna berry juice.* Her hand shook a little more than usual, she noticed, as she dropped the paper on the side table. She swallowed the rest of the bitter brew quickly, burning her tongue, and glanced around the room to find where the Resuscitation Crew would be waiting. Against the opposite wall she noticed a large mirror next to a door. Maeve quickly averted her eyes in case it were rude to look at them.

The room seemed to be getting darker, as if a cloth shroud was being drawn around her eyes, closing her vision and dimming the light. Her thoughts diminished and rattled around in her head that had suddenly become too large and they were lost in the extra space. She set the tea cup on the side table.

“I’m doing this for you, Mama,” she whispered. “I shouldn’t have let you die alone. I should have forgiven you. I was bad, so I drank my tea.” Her thoughts were congealing, moving like cold honey. She looked up towards the faux scene of her childhood, barely visible through the gray fog drifting over her sight. Her limbs felt cold and heavy. She wasn’t getting up from this chair anytime soon. It was time for a sleep. “Forgive me,” she whispered. Maeve felt her heart turn to stone in her chest, and then it ceased.

When the Resuscitation Crew came in they were subdued. This time were no rude jokes at the expense of the recently deceased They gently laid the old woman out, mindful of her delicate, papery skin as they injected her system with the healing nanos.

When Maeve came back to herself, it was quietly. She simply inhaled and opened her eyes. She barely spoke, answering the questions they asked without volunteering conversation. She thanked each of them before she left, promising to leave them each a generous tip at the front desk on her way out. She refused their offer to escort her, saying she preferred solitude to sort her thoughts.

Azrael was still at the desk when Maeve arrived back at the lobby. The old woman busied herself with making sure each technician was given a tip, and she insisted that Azrael also receive a gratuity.

“Did you find that death resolved anything for you?” asked Azrael. Maeve shook her head no.

"I guess I didn't really expect it to," she said. "But I had hoped. I wasted all my chances long ago." Azrael looked genuinely pained for her elderly client.

"We can only have so many second chances during life," said Azrael. "Even here there's a limit." Maeve took the young girl's hand and kissed it as her eyes teared up. "Good-bye, dear."

Maeve had her return trip already arranged and waiting. She climbed into the car quietly and spoke not a word during the trip. Upon arrival, she thanked the driver and paid, including a generous tip for him as well. She took the elevator up to her tiny apartment and went inside. Leaving the lights off, she set down her tiny bundle of spare clothes, unused, and looked out of her window.

This scene, she knew, was real. Her apartment window looked out on more windows, a wall of lit rectangles, set in the building next to hers. Behind each window, she realized, was a stranger. They all lived so close, were they not divided by brick and glass they could probably touch fingertips across the expanse. Sometimes they saw each other through the open blinds, eyes meeting briefly before their gazes averted. Despite their physical proximity, they were still strangers. Maeve realized that was her fault as much as theirs. *Someone had to say hello first,* she thought. *Someone had to forgive first.*

Maeve went to her tiny kitchen and poured herself a mug of hot water from the tap. She reached in her pocket and pulled out her second teabag. She didn't need to read the ingredients on the back this time. She knew it would do. She sat down with her mug of hot water and popped her tea bag in, letting it steep while she watched the windows of her nameless neighbors.

"Someone has to love first," she said to the empty room. "It could have been me." Maeve drink her tea slowly as evening closed in.

Take Out

"Pay attention," snapped the instructor. Each group of potential new drivers was the same—unruly and stupid. The group of final year students indulged him with their eyes, but their thoughts were obviously on the six compact cars parked at the edge of the light in an otherwise dark room.

They were in the basement of the Bitter Suites, a hotel that specialized in the singular experience of death, perfect for new driver experiences. He always started his orientations with the room black so his students could focus on him, not the surroundings. It also gave time for the volunteer bodies to get in place before they began. A mousy girl with a washed out complexion and pale orange hair raised her hand. He nodded to her, bracing himself for teenage angst or sarcasm, or both.

"If you don't take this perspective orientation you don't get personal transportation privileges, right?" She was chewing on the thumbnail of her other hand. "Are we really going to have to kill people?" She looked nervous. He warmed to her genuine concern. Before he could answer, Dillon, an over-sized repeat attender, piped in.

"Tons," he said. "That was the best part last time I did this." The instructor narrowed his eyes at Dillon. He remembered this kid.

"You probably shouldn't admit that you failed Correct Perspective last time." Dillon curled up a lip in a smile that wasn't meant to be friendly. If Dillon failed this time, he only got one more shot before he was doomed to a life of public transit. The instructor didn't see that attitude going anywhere except on the Potential Deviant lists. He was ready to fail him now. The girl with pale skin bit her lip and swallowed nervously. The instructor addressed the girl.

"Yes, to get a proper perspective you have to kill people. Here at the Bitter Suites it's not a big deal, though." He pointed to a button camera on the ceiling overhead. "One of the best resuscitator crews here is waiting a monitor away to step in and fix everyone. And remember…" The instructor paused for effect and looked at all of them individually. A half dozen young faces looked back at him, rapt at his words. He loved it.

"Everyone who dies here today volunteered for this. They are being compensated." Dillon just grinned for no reason. The kid was warped, that was clear. The instructor debated just failing him now, but knew he had to follow protocol or the kid would just appeal. Kids were just too smart these days. He blamed the apps. With legalese everywhere, they didn't even have to research anymore.

"Does everyone understand the point of this?" he asked. The group remained mute, eyes fixated on the cars behind him. Their eagerness was palpable, only the redhead girl seemed hesitant. By contrast, Dillon was overeager. The kid was actually licking his lips in anticipation. The instructor tried not to show his disgust, despite his feelings. "The point of this is to experience the consequences of driving mistakes in an emotionally real way. It will make you better drivers." As usual, there was no reaction to the most important point of his lecture.

"Okay then, choose your cars and let's play. Remember, all the cars are speed-capped at 30 miles per hour, so you can't get into too much trouble." The teenagers surged past him before he'd barely finished. He always thought it made more sense to make all the cars the same color to avoid this rush,

Black, he thought. *All the cars should be black. That would avoid all the last minute scuffle for the red car.*

Once the cars had been chosen with a minimum of infighting and the students belted themselves in, he went around for final checks. The mousy girl was named Sara, it said on her application. He peeked into her car to find her gripping the steering wheel with white knuckles. Her car, appropriately, was gray.

"Hey, don't be afraid," he told her. "Try to hit at least one person so you can pass with proper perspective." Her eyes darted up to meet his before locking back onto the dash. She shook her head.

"I'm not afraid," she said. "I'm an empath. This is going to hurt me as much as them." The instructor felt instant pity. Empaths had the right perspective from birth. Forcing them to take orientations like this was cruel. They should have the right to refuse. He gave her a genuine look of concern.

"If this gets too much for you, signal me and I'll get you out. Try to hit someone early and get it over with. I'll let you wait outside." She nodded, paler than when she came in. He could already see the tears clustering in the corner of her eyes.

"Hey, can we get on with this?" Dillon's voice rang out in the shadows, a few cars away. The instructor decided he actually hated the kid. He'd always had a problem with people that enjoyed pain. *Fantastic,* he thought. *I have an empath and an apath in the same orientation. Someone really screwed up the screening.* He took his radio out.

"Let's get going," he said to it. "Lights on."

High above them, lights switched on, eliminating the dark and temporarily blinding the drivers. This was also part of his plan. It gave him a few minutes to get off the floor while their eyes adjusted. He headed towards the exit, walking backwards when he neared the door so he could watch.

As expected, the students were blinking and peering through their windshields at the room, revealed so abruptly. The basement of the Bitter Suites always surprised first-timers with how huge it was. Like an industrial cathedral, the lowest level was designed for large scale experiences. Ceilings scaled at least three stories, blinding the eyes with the massive flood lights that hung there like flying saucers from an old sci-fi movie. He backed against the exit, safe now.

The first car, Dillon's of course, was already moving. Beyond the cars was a mocked up street scene. Large mats that simulated asphalt had been rolled out to make streets. Stoplights and storefronts formed a subsection of a town. Volunteer bodies were already moving around, some of them more hesitantly than others. On his side, he could see a volunteer hiding behind one of the storefront facades.

"Remind the volunteers that they don't get compensated if they don't get killed," he said into the radio. Thirty seconds later he watched the volunteer bend her head and put a hand up to her ear, listening. After another ten seconds she nodded, spoke a few words and reluctantly went around the storefront to cross the street.

Meanwhile, more cars had started moving. Dillon's red car was already on the imitation roadway, driving down the center line and veering towards the volunteers on the sidewalk. The instructor pulled the mic off the wall next to the door and flipped on the loudspeaker.

"Dillon, the idea is to at least pretend like you are following road rules. Each of you only needs to hit one person to pass." Dillon's car swerved onto the sidewalk and narrowly missed a volunteer who jumped, in spite of their purpose. "If you kill too many people, I will consider you to have failed Correct Perspective." Dillon yelled something and waved from the car. The instructor flipped off the mic and hung it back on the wall.

"I'm not passing that boy," he muttered to himself.

Predictably, the gray car was the last to enter the mock town. The instructor could picture Sara inside, face already wet from tears as she prepared to go against her nature. If a car could move reluctantly, hers did.

The instructor's cousin had been an empath, and they'd grown up together. The cousin had been institutionalized, at his own request, shortly after they graduated. Now he existed in an emotionally minimalist world, insulated from media, in order to stay sane. *I should visit him soon,* he thought.

Dillon's car surged ahead. The volunteers dodged his overly aggressive attempts to hit them, despite their training. Dillon's car ran into a storefront and it swayed precariously. The instructor was about to reach for the microphone again when the first body fell.

A pale blue car smacked into a woman crossing the street. The instructor couldn't remember the driver's name as he notated time and reaction. The car stopped, and then the driver's side flew open. A boy jumped out and ran to the woman. He cradled her on the ground, body language expressing remorse. The instructor scribbled *pass* next to the time of hit.

Dillon's car had stopped and the big boy was standing, half out of his car, yelling something. He popped back and slammed the door before gunning the engine. His little red car took off down the roadway, heading for the boy and the woman huddled in front of the blue car. The instructor's stomach knotted as he reached for the mic again.

Before he could mash the talk button, Dillon's car smashed into the two on the ground, clipping the blue car so that it spun sideways. The instructor saw the boy's head impact the bumper before the car rolled over both of them. There was a flash of Dillon's face, laughing maniacally and then the car was racing past.

"Dillon!" the instructor screamed into the mic. The speaker system shrieked with him, feedback striking eardrums like audible lightening. In the town, a little yellow car was trying to turn around as the red car sped towards it. "Stop now!" The instructor yelled, and again feedback rang out, contorting his voice into a mechanical scream.

The red car smashed into the driver's side door, pushing it sideways into a light post. The light post toppled, the bolts that held it to the floor no match for the heavy impact. Dillon's car reversed, slamming into another storefront, causing it to buckle.

"Shut them down!" The instructor yelled, this time into his radio. Thirty miles an hour may as well have been a hundred to a mind bent on destruction.

The driver of the yellow car opened the door and rolled out. Dillon hit the gas, crushing the boy between the two vehicles. Alarms went off and red lights started flashing high overhead. All the cars stopped moving except Dillon's. Volunteers started scattering, running for the exits. "Resuscitators, now!" screamed the instructor.

Side doors along the far edges of the vast room flew open and the medical geeks started running towards the mess. Volunteers ran the other way, eager to forego any compensation to escape what had turned into a nightmare. Dillon's car backed up and started up again, down the middle of the road and to the edge of the fake buildings. The instructor realized the kid was going for the resuscitators.

"Fail!" he screamed. "You fail! Stop!" Dillon couldn't hear him from this distance, and it was doubtful he would have listened anyway. The boy was bent on mayhem, mad face leering over the steering wheel, foot mashed on the gas. Too late, the group running to help noticed the rogue car aiming at them. They all stopped, and then started trying to run different directions. One dropped his bag, causing the person behind him to trip over it, sprawling. The red car was nearly on them, prepared to mow down the scrambling group of bodies.

From the side, a gray car appeared from nowhere and ran directly into the driver's side door. Dillon's car skidded sideways ten feet before both cars stopped. All movement ceased as everyone tried to process the new situation. Dillon's door flung open, and he half fell out. His mouth gaped as he yelled something to the driver in the gray car. Sara started backing up, slowly at first and then picking up speed. Dillon had stumbled around his car by now, waving a pudgy fist at her car and yelling. He stumbled towards her, clumsy aggression giving him a lopsided, almost skipping gait.

Chaos took over. The remaining two student drivers had exited their cars and were running for the outskirts. The resuscitators had scattered. Not used to being targets, they were fleeing in all directions. The instructor was screaming incoherently into the mic and loud speaker simultaneously, creating a cacophony of discordant feedback. In the middle of it all, the gray car stopped backing up.

Dillon continued running, his helter skelter gait evening out as he regained his balance. Sara didn't stand a chance against the hulking, meat-fisted monster coming toward her. The instructor dropped everything and started running towards them.

Dillon was closing in when the gray car started moving. Tires squealed against the smooth floor as the driver punched the acceleration too quickly. Catching traction, the little car lurched forward, quickly gaining speed, heading straight for Dillon.

He stumbled and stopped, unsure, and then the gray car was plowing into him. Catching him mid-thigh, he slammed face first into the hood before flipping backward over the entire car and slamming into the floor behind. The gray car slid to a stop. Again, time stopped in shock. Before anyone could react, Sara yanked the car in reverse and sped back the way she'd come, nearly flipping the small car as she bumped over Dillon's prostrate form.

Twice more the little gray car ran over the boy, each time bouncing the vehicle high like a miniature, macabre monster truck. The third time, Sara stopped and the instructor ran to her door, expecting to find a trembling, sobbing girl. Instead, Sara sat, dry-eyed, on her phone. The instructor stopped, confused.

"Legalities for vehicular manslaughter, with a self defense vigilantism angle please," she said to her phone.

"Understood. A legal expert will be contacting you shortly," the phone answered. Sara looked up at the instructor. He was leaning on her door with both hands, panting and confused. She smiled, and a hint of the old Sara passed across her face like a nervous shadow and evaporated.

"I think he cured me of my empathy," she said. "I actually *wanted* to hurt him. I've never felt that before." Her eyes glowed with excitement, and the instructor felt a cold fist slowly knot up in his bowels. Across the expanse of room, side doors were flying open and medical techs were rushing towards the mayhem. Even Azreal came down to survey the disaster. The phone's dispassionate voice spoke again.

"Sara, please refrain from any emotional commentary or a legal expert may not be able to assist you. A team is en route to meet you at the Bitter Suites." A few feet away, Dillon lay, a pile of meat on the slick floor. Sara leaned forward over the dashboard, taking it in, and grinned.

"I'm completely cured of empathy," she said. "This feels amazing." The instructor wasn't sure if she was talking to herself, Dillon's bleeding body or him. He felt sick.

"Sara, I must caution you again. Please refrain from any emotional commentary," said the phone.

"Okay, sorry," said Sara. She was looking at what was left of Dillon with a wicked grin.

The instructor didn't believe her.

Popcorn

I walked into the lobby of the Bitter Suites and saw her. Azreal looked the same as the first time I saw her. Her hair, almost black at the roots lightened into a honey blonde at the tips. The effect wasn't unnatural, like she needed a root touch up. The effect was more like a twilight sky glowing towards morning. She looked up at me and frowned.

"I don't have you in my books," she said. I wandered over to her behind the desk. Even though we'd spoken on a near monthly basis for the past three years, we'd never moved beyond a mild familiarity. Not because I wouldn't want that. It just never happened.

"My friend booked me in," I answered. "He might have mistakenly put it under his name."

"You're dying too much," she said. "It's against our policy. I won't book you more than once a month. Death isn't meant to be this frequent." I smiled and leaned on the counter, towards her. I was trying to see the names in her book because I'd forgotten who I'd conned into booking for me. She lifted her book so I couldn't read it.

"It has been over a month for me," I told her. "Look it up in your records." Her eyes flicked back and forth on the page and then up to the digital wall calendar.

"A month to the day." She looked at me and raised an eyebrow. "Seriously?"

"Okay, so this seems a little sneaky," I said. "I know I can't book another death for a one month period, but I also know it's so the medi-nanos don't start repairing themselves and mess you up. I waited a month. I know how busy the Bitter Suites gets. Having someone book for me speeds us all along. You want my money, right?" She looked at me through narrowed eyes.

"You have a problem. You're becoming a junkie." I threw my hands up in the air dramatically.

"Whoa! Is this how you treat faithful clients? Call me a death junkie? I should complain to management." She wasn't impressed.

"I am the management," she said. She leaned forward across the counter and took my hands into hers. Her touch felt like the muscle rub they wipe all over athletes—hot and cold at the same time. I wondered what she would be like to kiss.

"The rules are made to keep you safe," she said. "You're so involved in killing yourself that you forget to live. Bitter Suites is supposed to be here to enrich your life, not sap it." Her eyes seemed to light up on their own, as if they were back lit. I could see summer in them, the perfect kind of day you only ever have as a kid. I wanted to stay there, savoring that feeling. "Go home," she said.

Home. That thought melted my summer day memory like a lost popsicle, sticky and wasted on the sidewalk. Home for me was a gray, one room flat down the street. The windows were all painted over, but the streetlights still seemed to sneak their way through the scratches to keep me up at night. My neighbors were all nut jobs in the middle of DNA breakdowns. Sometimes I find clots of nasty, wet hair stuck to the hall walls, and I want to puke. Home, to me, is a dead place. I'm only alive when I'm here. I jerked my hands away.

"Are you going to honor my booking or not?" Azreal sighed and looked back at the book before looking back up at me. "I suppose legally I have to. What package was booked?" I swear, she looked a little like she was going to cry. I felt bad, but I needed this. I needed this.

"It was the circus fetish package, with assistant," I answered. "Bring on the bizarro!" My stomach did a somersault. The circus deaths were considered kind of extreme to most recreational suiciders, but I was an aficionado by now. Since my very first experience, I was hooked on the rush a renewed life brings on. Colors are brighter, everything tastes amazing and even my gross neighbors seem tolerable. Azreal didn't say anything else. She checked me into her log book, retrieved the keycard and slid it across the counter to me. I snatched it quick before she could change her mind.

"I'm good to go! See you on the flipside." I grinned at her, backing my way to the elevators. I held my keycard up and used it to blow her a kiss.

"You know you say that almost every time," Azreal said. "It's getting a little old, and so are you." She turned her back on me. I stood still for a moment as sadness flooded me. I felt like a child that had lost something, but I couldn't remember what had been so precious.

If the girl behind the counter had turned back to me then, I might have hesitated, but Azreal remained facing away, stubbornly. Whatever was wilting my wonder, I knew the fix was just a few floors below.

"Then I guess I'm just off to the circus then," I said to her back, and I turned my own self away. The elevator opened and I stepped in and hit the button for the basement. That's where the real action at the Bitter Suites is.

I'd gone all out on this suicide. I may have a crappy life, but I'd had some nitro deaths. Life passed me by in a featureless, flat miasma until the days I died. Like a beam of Technicolor light cutting through an abandoned warehouse, those were the days that flooded me with meaning and clarity. Joy, tangible and sweet, drenched everything and continued to radiate. Eventually, it always faded. In its absence, living seemed even more dull.

The elevator door slid open and I walked out into the cold, concrete hall. No frills in the basement. It was all business with cement block wall and a janitor's cart at one end. Not many people took on the large scale experiences the basement could handle. I read somewhere that the ceiling is three stories high. I walked up to a pair of metal double doors and pushed my way in. Looking up at the trapeze and nets swaying high overhead, I could believe it. I stepped in and let the big metal doors close behind me.

As usual, the Bitter Suites had gone all out to create an authentic experience. A long, wooden pole was set in the center of the room to hold up heavy folds of canvas tent in red and white. Nets, rope and tiny platforms swayed above me. A spotlight flooded the large, raised ring dominating the center of the room. Empty bleachers, coils of rope and storage lockers littered the edges of the light. Curtains of the thick, striped canvas hung from the ceiling. High above it all were the massive lights, hanging in midair like UFOs. A jolt of anticipation went through my nerves like lightning as adrenaline flooded my system. Kill me already!

At the opposite end of the ring the curtains moved and a woman in a scanty, ringleader outfit emerged. Her red sequined coat and tails hugged every curve. Fishnet stockings, patent leather knee boots and a little top hat pinned into her cartoon-bright red hair completed the look. She saw me from across the tent, heavy, green eye shadow framed her eyes, and nodded.

"Ready?" she called out. I grinned, all goofy and excited, but I didn't care what she thought of me. I was paying everything I had for this experience. I'd even redeemed my vocational vouchers. Screw moving out of my maintenance job. I had finally realized it didn't matter what I did on a day-to-day basis. I was only alive and happy when I was dying. I sold my future for this night. I closed my eyes, breathing in the scent of sawdust and sand. This was the moment I savored—when time stopped for me and all the crap rest of my life seemed inconsequential.

"Ready," I said finally. I kept my eyes closed, waiting. Electric silence, and then carnival music and laugh track cheers filled the basement area. The smell of fresh popcorn wafted towards me.

"Ladies and gentlemen! Are you ready?" My eyes flew open to see my sexy ringmaster striding into the ring with a microphone. From behind the curtain a half dozen clowns came out of nowhere. They cavorted into the ring with somersaults and backflips. One of them started chasing the other clowns with a chainsaw. He wore a hockey mask. Nothing at the Bitter Suites was fake when it came to death, so I assumed it was real.

The other clowns scattered before him, comically sprawling on their faces and doing silly flips as they pretended to trip. These guys were good enough they should have their own show beyond the suicide circuit. I couldn't help laughing and clapping.

Chainsaw clown took notice of me and started running my way. Even though it seems counterproductive, I couldn't help taking off when he got close. Fight or flight is impossible to turn off, I had found, even when your intention is to lose.

"Holy crap!" I yelled, laughing. The guy was seriously scary. I ran up to the ring mistress and bowed, low. "At your service, ma'am."

"We have a volunteer from the audience," she yelled into the microphone. She grabbed my hand and lifted it over her head, champion style. Canned cheers erupted all around us. My eyes scanned the shadowed bleachers. They were still empty, but who cares? This was my fantasy. I lifted my other hand into the air and made a victory fist pump. The crowd got louder. She dropped my hand and the crowd silenced.

"My good sir," said the ring mistress. "Are you ready to entertain the masses gathered here, even at risk of your own life?" Another thrill went through me and I could feel goosebumps raise up on my skin. I looked into her eyes, each gray iris framed in long, nylon lashes.

"Yes," I said.

"Sir, the people gathered here today can't hear you," she was yelling into the mic, even though we both knew there was no one here but us and the clowns. "I asked if you were ready to entertain the people of this audience, even at risk to your own life. What do you say, good sir?"

"Yes!" I screamed, throwing my head back and uttering primal affirmation to the ceiling. "Yes!" She lowered the microphone and leaned in close. She smelled like tobacco and sweat.

"Then let's get started," she said, purring low into my ear. My insides quivered. She raised the microphone to her lips with a smile.

"Clowns!" she yelled again into the microphone. I jumped in spite of myself. "Please escort our daring hero to the high wires!" Behind me, Chainsaw clown started revving his motor. I spun around to see him approaching, blue face paint showing through the eyes of his hockey mask. He was ridiculously scary. I ran.

I get that I shouldn't be afraid of being chopped up by a chainsaw, given that I came here for an exciting death, and I'd already been done by chainsaw last year. I'd accepted a future of shit jobs in exchange for this experience and there was no way these guys were getting an early night.

I ran screaming like a little girl around the ring. The clowns were all banding together, trying to trip me with their oversized shoes and throwing things as I went past. They started chanting, and even though I'd gotten a little jaded about dying, I was feeling real fear.

"Chop him up! Chop him up!" The canned crowd was cheering and screaming with the clowns. The chainsaw clown had nearly caught up with me a few times, but, lucky for me, his big shoes slowed him down.

Not lucky for me, I was getting tired. I stumbled as I tried to hop over a beach ball and went down face first into the sawdust. I caught a whiff of acrid animal urine. Like I said, the Bitter Suites was top notch for authenticity.

A mechanical whir filled my ears, and as I tried to turn, I felt my clothes and flesh twist together as the chain saw took a nibble from my side. I screamed, garbled, and spit sawdust and drool as I propelled myself forward. Ahead of me, a rope ladder was attached to the center pole. I'd been trying to prolong the chase, but I think the staff was getting impatient. Up the ladder I scrambled.

The crowd went wild. I knew they were all pre-recorded cheers, but it still made me feel like some kind of valiant superhero as I escaped certain death. My ribs throbbed where the chainsaw had bit in. Half way up I looked down, panting. The clowns and the ring mistress were all gathered around, watching me climb. As soon as I stopped, the clown with the chainsaw made like he was going to saw the pole in two. I cooperated and finished the climb.

At the top, I sat down to rest on the small platform. The only way off was to walk a tightrope or climb back down. I didn't see how the tight rope was going to happen. I'm not that talented. I was pretty sure I hadn't ordered this. There is no way I even know how to step on that thing.

"Ladies and gentleman!" The voice of the ring mistress boomed even louder from up here. I could see big speakers set in the corners of the ceiling. "Please, turn your attention to the platform high above our heads and witness our brave volunteer walk the Thread of Flame!" Drumbeats and trumpets blared out in the room as a symphonic storm.

A woman in a gold lamé bikini walked into the ring. In her hand she carried an ornate, wooden bow. At her hip was a quiver of arrows. The clowns were all entertaining themselves with faints and swoons at her good looks. Chainsaw Clown knelt before her, placing his blade at her feet like a knight. I watched, confused. Into the ring came a small boy, painted in gold. He held aloft a lighted torch. I didn't order this at all.

"Hail, Prometheus, bringing the gift of fire!" said the ring leader. The girl in the golden bikini pulled an arrow from her quiver and held it out to the boy. Suddenly, I was a fortune teller and I could predict the future.

"Crap!" I said out loud, and I looked around wildly for any kind of escape besides the rope. If I tried that, I would just fall right to my death with no more foreplay.

"Stop," I yelled down. "This is going too fast! It's supposed to be epic—I paid for this!"

The archer girl placed an arrow against her bow string and pulled it taught, aiming at me. I struggled to stand up. The boy lifted his torch, setting the end aflame. She let go, and the arrow came straight at me and embedded into the platform with a thunk.

The heat was almost immediate. Yes, I was here to have a death but pain was still pain, and no one could just stand in fire and passively burn to death.

"Assholes!" I yelled down as I hopped back and forth on the platform. Flame was already licking around the wood, seeking a taste of me. I'd have to try the rope. If I made it, these suckers were going to be stuck here all night killing me. Then I was turning in a complaint.

I didn't get far. I set one foot out onto the rope, and then it just fell away in a trail of ash. The wood under my other foot cracked, knocking my head into the pole and then it too gave way. Down I went, falling in a shower of ember and ash, to meet the concrete floor below.

The crunch I made when I hit was pretty extreme. There was some sort of pop, which I think may have been my skull, but then all sound and sense went wonky. The ring mistress, the clowns and the golden bikini gathered around to look at me. Good for me, I was still hanging in there.

"Not… done…" I managed to gasp. That was it though. My lungs were punctured and there was such a riot of pain so I couldn't tell what else might be going on. At least I was getting my money's worth from the resuscitators.

This death sucked.

"Actually, you are done," said gold bikini. "Azreal said this is for your own good. You've got a problem." She notched another arrow and pulled back, the arrow tip a foot away from my left eye. My brain was so scrambled by this point I don't think I understood what she was doing until it was too late. The arrow left the bow. In a split second it was buried in what was left of my brain.

I woke up, sore and sad on the lobby couch. Azreal was sitting next to me. She looked as sad and sorry as I felt. As soon as she noticed my eyes open, her look hardened.

"I hate to inform you, but you have been banned from the Bitter Suites," she said. My brain must have still been repairing, because I couldn't understand what she was trying to say.

"What?" I asked. I'd never seen her out from behind the counter before. Her outer thigh was against my side, and I was acutely aware of the touch.

"This is an intervention," she said. Her eyes softened as her brow furrowed in concern. She leaned forward and placed her hand on my cheek. The gesture was so intimate and strange, I was shocked to silence. "You can't do this anymore. You have gotten addicted and you're only living to die. I have to ban you." The words started clicking and making sense.

"What? I'm one of your best customers," I said. I struggled to sit up. "You can't ban me! No one else has the tech for this. You guys corner the market on resurrection." Two big goons appeared out of my peripheral vision like ghosts. They stood behind Azreal, communicating a warning without uttering a word. I didn't care. I pushed Azreal away from me and sat all the way up. I could still feel soft, painful spots where I was healing. My head ached.

"If you ban me, I have nothing left to live for. Seriously!" Azreal looked pained, like this hurt her like it did me, and I felt a pang of guilt. This was because I'd cheated the system and gotten a friend to make my reservation too early. "I'll wait longer from now on. Please, believe me! I'll have nothing left, Azreal."

"And that's exactly why I have to ban you," she said. "You've gotten so hooked on death that you've closed everything else down. The Bitter Suites can't be responsible for suicide abuse." Azreal stood up, signaling the interview was over.

"No!" I yelled and slammed my hand down on the couch. The gesture seemed pathetic, especially since the Beef Brothers scooped me up like an angry toddler and started carrying me outside. I couldn't believe I was being expelled from the Bitter Suites.

"Do you know how much money I've spent here? I'll find a way around this, you know I will." Suddenly, Azreal was in my face as they carried me out the door.

"There is only one way around this. The path you are choosing only leads one way. Turn back." She smiled at me then, soft and gentle. I was reminded how I had a crush on her the first time I'd seen her. She leaned forward and kissed me on the forehead. Weird, but I kind of wanted to cry just then.

"You'll be back," she said. "But only for a minute before you're removed." And then I was outside. The goons must have called a cab because suddenly I was being folded into it. The full impact hit me minutes later. I'd given up my future prospects for this experience. It was supposed to charge me up for a lifetime.

Instead, I felt no redeeming rush of joy. Everything was flat and washed in gray. My future stretched before me with no hope of anything better. A shitty flat awaited me. A shitty job was beyond that. The one bright spot, the rush of a good death, was now no longer in the picture. Azreal was right. This was no longer recreational. I needed it.

I pressed my forehead against the glass, watching cold rain trickle down without touching me—just like life.

I had to fix this.

Mochi and Umeboshi

A well dressed man and his wife came into the lobby and stopped inside the door. They didn't seem to belong there. They looked conservative, unlike the usual death devotees that populated the Bitter Suites. The woman, navy blue pencil skirt and tailored jacket, pointed to Azrael, waiting behind the lobby desk, and spoke in a murmur. The man followed her gesture, gave a curt nod, and stepped forward.

"We have an appointment for our two girls," he said. "Mochi and Umeboshi." Azreal looked up at the clock on the wall and then down at her appointment book. The woman had walked up behind him. She looked nervous and uncomfortable. She glanced around the lobby in discrete peeks before turning her attention to the girl behind the desk.

"We call them Mochi and Ume," said the woman. "Sweet Rice and Sour Plum." Her husband pursed his lips and went on as if she hadn't spoken.

"We have an appointment for them." Azreal studied the couple for a moment, trying to assess their intentions. "I see the girls are both legal as of today. Is this a surprise for them?" The woman nodded and smiled.

"It is to bond them," said the man. "They were born together. They should be close. This is their last chance to connect as sisters before adulthood."

"This is why we call them Mochi and Ume," said the woman. "Mochi is full of love and laughter. Ume is sour. Just a small bit of her bitterness goes a long way." She flashed a quick smile and then it vanished just as fast. Azreal could see where the girls had gotten their opposing personalities.

"So, they have an appointment?" The father was brisk and efficient. "They will be here any minute unless I tell the driver otherwise." He pulled his phone from a breast pocket and tapped in his unlock code.

"Yes, said Azreal. "Their appointment is confirmed." She found the correct keycard and slid them across the counter. The man returned the phone to his pocket and picked up the keycard. "They may go directly to the room when they arrive."

"Good," he said. He turned his back on Azreal and walked to the center of the lobby to stand in front of the entrance. His wife gave an apologetic smile before following him. They both stood still, waiting.

The next five minutes crawled by with Azreal trying not to look at the living mannequins that had taken residence in her lobby. The woman had moved closer to take his arm and then they both became motionless until a car pulled up outside.The woman made a small coo of relief as a driver opened the door.

A pretty girl exited the car, grinning with excitement. She thanked the driver before turning back to gesture dramatically. She turned to look up at the building, eyes casting their way past the Bitter Suites' lighted marquee to the 13th floor above and then she clapped her hands like a little girl before bursting into the lobby.

"The Bitter Suites! Are you going to let us die?" she asked. She rushed to her parents and squeezed them both, oblivious to any response. The mother brushed her daughter's hair back and kissed her cheek. Even the father grinned down at her. "This is going to be so amazing!"

Another girl exited the car. She ignored the driver's offered hand. Azreal watched her through the glass as she too scanned the hotel's facade. Her neck craned backwards, seeking the top floor. Calmly, she looked back down, through the glass doors where she could see her parents and Mochi hugging. She watched, expressionless, and then her lips peeled back to reveal perfect teeth.

There was no joy or humor in this expression. The grin was crooked and twisted, more snarl than smile. Her eyes lit up with a fevered shine, glinting in the fading light. A shadow slipped over Ume's face as she watched her family hugging, and then whatever emotion she had let play across her face was shuttered. She pushed through the door.

"Ume! I wondered where you were!" The mother disengaged herself from Mochi's embrace. "Do you like your birthday surprise?" She dropped her arms to her side and fiddled with the seams of her skirt. Mochi was oblivious to the emotional chill that emanated from her sister.

"Umeboshi! We get to have our first grown-up death!" She ran the few steps to her sister in an very un-grownup manner and hugged her as well. Like a wriggling puppy, her excitement was impossible to stifle. Ume didn't protest the embrace, but she didn't respond either. Mochi's natural joy bubbled up from some happy well inside her, independent.

"Are we dying separately or together?" asked Ume over her sister's shoulder. Her father pulled the keycard from his pocket and held it up.

"One room, two deaths," he said. Ume shook her sister off and walked to her father. She plucked the card from his hand and looked at the room number. "The penthouse. Thank you, Father. Thank you, Mother. We'll enjoy this present." Her voice was flat.

"Umeboshi, please don't be so distant. You are a woman. This is a special day." Her mother reached forward without taking a step, bending at the waist, and touched Ume's arm. The girl looked down at her mother's hand as if it confused her, and then back up and into her mother's eyes.

"I am very excited, Mother," said Ume in the same, flat tone. She smiled then, the same, fevered dark expression that Azreal had witnessed earlier. Her mother dropped her hand and stood straight.

"Happy birthday then, dears," she said. She looked up at her husband. "Shall we sit and wait?" He nodded. Taking her arm, he escorted her to a sitting area off to one side without another word to the girls. Undeterred, Mochi grabbed her sister's arm and pulled her towards the elevators. Ume allowed herself to be pulled in. As the doors closed, they watched their mother half raise up from the couch. Their father, who had settled back into his mannequin state, looked up at her surprised.

"I love you, my sweet Mochi!" she called. Her eyes glittered wetly in the lobby lamps. She caught sight of Ume, staring back with a dark expression. "And Ume..." The elevator doors closed, cutting off her words. The girls were alone in the elevator. They were passing the sixth floor before either of them spoke.

"She loves you too," said Mochi. Ume made no reply.

"I know she didn't say it, but I'm sure she meant it," Mochi continued. She was smiling but the effect was less sweet in the dim light of the elevator. There was a dangerous sharpness to her, like a kitten playing. "They would probably love you more if you weren't always so gloomy." Still, Ume said nothing. They passed the 11th floor. The elevator stopped moving at the 13th floor.

"No wonder no one likes you," said Mochi as the doors slid open. She stepped out and whistled. Ume followed her. They were in a lush waiting room. Their shoes sank deep into the thick, crimson carpet. The wallpaper was a textured cream color with geometric designs of pressed gold foil. Double doors of polished zebra wood and brass were before them. Ume stepped forward and slid the keycard in the lock. The door popped open with a click. Both girls exhaled.

They were no strangers to wealth. Their parents had always provided them with the best of everything, but their parents were highly conservative—never ostentatious. The walls of their house were cream with white trim. The most exotic item in their house had been the dining room table, made of burled wood, but even that was accompanied by beige upholstered chairs and white dishes. This room was completely different from anything they had experienced.

Like the door, the furniture was made of zebra wood and brass. The lush carpet continued into the penthouse apartment bringing a riot of warmth and color to the two girls who had grown up without it. A red, velour fainting couch could be seen through an open door. Across it was a throw in leopard print. Ume walked through to inspect the next room.

It was set up to be a private theater. A large screen was set into the wall. A comfortable, half-circle couch faced it. Heavy red curtains were hung along the wall. Ume walked to them and groped in the heavy folds until she found what she was looking for—a glass door that led to the balcony she had seen from below. She went to the rail and looked down. Satisfied, she went back inside, leaving the door open behind her.

She rejoined her sister in the main room. All the furniture had been removed and replaced by a low, Japanese style table in the middle. Two cushions sat on either side of the table. A kimono was folded neatly on each cushion. On the table was a pot of tea, two small cups with no handles and two short blades. Beneath each blade was a small card. Beneath each kimono was a braided red cord.

"Looks like a party," said Mochi. "A boring party." She walked to the small table and chose a kimono. It was white silk with pink and red cherry blossoms embroidered across it. She draped it over her shoulders. "But at least we get to keep these." Ume came over and unfolded the other one.

It was black silk with golden orange chrysanthemums embroidered across it. She held it up to her face, feeling the smooth material against her skin. With her face covered, she gave a secret smile and inhaled the scent of incense.

"They had to include one for you," she heard her sister say. Her smile was lost in the folds of silk. She let the robe fall to drape over her arm. Her face was as expressionless as always.

"I know," she said. "I just want to make sure it's been laundered." She bent over and picked up the card and read while Mochi stripped and replaced her outfit with the kimono. She turned before a mirrored wall to admire herself. The clothes she had worn were discarded in a pile.

"The blades are called *tanto*," said Ume. "We're supposed to slice our stomachs from left to right." She read on, and then bent over to pick up the cord. "We are supposed to tie our knees together with this so we can die in a ladylike position." She raised her eyebrows and looked at her sister, dangling the cord. Mochi giggled.

"That's dumb. I thought we'd get something exciting, not some lame, traditional death." She rolled her eyes. "Leave it to lame, traditional parents." She turned away from the mirror and walked to the table to pick up the blade.

"I should just kill you. That would be exciting. Why do we have to kill ourselves?"

"I had the same thought before we even came upstairs," said Ume. A whisper of a smile played at the corners of her mouth. She dropped the card and picked up the other knife.

"I could finally get rid of you," said Mochi. "Just because we shared a womb doesn't mean we have to share a life."

"What we've shared can hardly be called a life," said Ume. "You've made sure to keep me pushed into the corner and out of your spotlight."

"You're still here," said Mochi. "So I haven't pushed hard enough, I guess. But just wishful thinking. Neither of us can kill the other permanently. The resuscitators will just bring us both back."

"I suppose you're right," said Ume. "But we could try." Mochi sniffed.

"You mean I could try. You've never beaten me at anything ever."

Ume just shrugged. "You're right, you'd win anyway." She tossed her kimono back onto it's cushion. "This is boring. Come see the movie screen in the next room. It's our own, personal theater."

"Really?" Mochi dropped her blade back onto the table and wandered into the next room. Ume followed.

"This is cool!" Mochi sat down on the half-circle couch. "Turn out the lights and let's see what they have." Ume obediently dimmed the lights while her sister turned on a small screen set into one end of the couch. She bent over the touchpad, making selections. In front of her the wall lit up and and music filled the room.

Behind her, Ume was smiling again. She walked up behind her sister on the couch and looked down at her bent form. In her hand, she still held her tanto. In a swift motion, she grabbed a handful of Mochi's hair and pulled her head back.

"Ow! Bitch!" Mochi's voice barely carried over the loud soundtrack that surrounded them. Upside down, she scowled at Ume and reached her hands up to release her hair from her sister's grip. Ume raised the tanto up over her sister and brought it down into her stomach, sinking the short blade to the hilt. She pulled hard to the right, twisting the knife as she cut. She let go, leaving the blade sunk into Mochi's abdomen.

Still holding her hair, she dragged her sister sideways off the couch, onto the floor and across the room. The white kimono was already soaked, the cherry blossoms vanishing in the bright blood. Ume pulled her sister onto the balcony and let go. Mochi doubled over, clutching the blade with one hand. The other she raised up to Ume. She pointed a shaking finger at her.

"Get... help...stupid...hurts"

Ume's face split open in a wide grin. Her eyes were wide with excitement.

"Mochi, guess what?" She started pulling her sister upright and pinned her hunched form against the railing.

"What..." gasped Mochi. Her mouth hung open slack and her eyes were dulling.

"I win," said Ume. She heaved her sister's body over the rail to drop freely until it met with the street, 13 floors below. She watched and savored the feeling of individuality that washed over her. She was no longer a twin. The night air smelled like freedom.

Ume walked back inside, through the loud theater room and into the main area. She picked up her black kimono as the mirrored wall split open. Several individuals in jumpsuits spilled out.

"Is she over the balcony? How did she fall?" someone asked Ume, but she didn't answer. She slipped the kimono over her clothes while the team rushed past her to the next room. She heard voices crackle over a radio.

"Get a team to the ground. She's outside!"

"We won't reach her in time..."

"Stick her anyways! We have to get her back up...!"

Ume walked back to the elevators, still smiling. She pressed the button to go downstairs and caught her reflection in the brass. It was distorted, but for the first time in her life, she saw only one reflection.

"Best birthday ever," she told it. The elevator doors opened, and she stepped inside as an only child.

Indigestion

"I'd like to apply for a job here as a resucitator." Azreal looked up in surprise at the man who stood before her counter. She hadn't heard him come in at all. He placed an envelope of papers in front of her.

"I am fully trained as a regular EMT with a certificate in NanoTech. I heard you had a few openings after..." He paused and gave Azreal a sympathetic smile before continuing. "After the recent unfortunate incident."

Azreal winced. She had understood that she couldn't hide news about the accident from the press, but she hadn't volunteered it either. The family had also been reluctant for any publicity, given that their surviving daughter would be the center of the media maelstrom. She had hoped lack of attention would make it go away.

"How did you hear about it?" asked Azreal. "And please, refer to it as an *accident* rather than an *incident*."

"In my circles, we keep tabs on that sort of thing." he said, nodding toward the envelope of credentials he had placed on the counter. Azreal took the envelope and opened it, spreading copies of certifications and his resume out on the table. She selected one of the papers and looked it over.

"Killian Grey. You've already filled out the application, I see." she said. "Can I ask how you came by this? Our recruiters only pass the company application on to the top graduates in the class."

"I admit, it was given to me," he answered. "I was second in my graduating class, as you can see. I thought it was worth a shot." He didn't bother to mention it hadn't been freely given. "This is my dream job."

"To be a resucitator?" asked Azreal, surprised. "I won't lie to you. Most MedTechs consider this a hostile work environment with high stress. Only our extremely competitive pay and benefits packages keep us fully staffed. Why do you want to join our team?" He leaned forward on the counter, infringing upon her personal space. She didn't mind.

"Call me crazy, but I see renewable death as a healthy thing," he said. "As an EMT I've gotten to see first hand how a near death experience can put everything in perspective for people. We scrabble around, wasting our precious days with petty worries and pains. Meanwhile, the big picture—life—passes over us on a big screen we hardly notice. Death brings that into focus. When I found out that Bitter Suites had the tech to control death I knew I wanted to be a part of that. Renewable death is life enrichment."

Azreal was charmed. When she had first opened the Bitter Suites, the public outcry had been bigger than anticipated. Pro-death groups had picketed the hotel for months and talk shows had taken up the Bitter Suites as a hot keyword to grab viewers. Everything from the decor to the highly secretive nanomeds that made resurrection possible were discussed in great detail by 'experts' Azreal had never heard of.

"We prefer to call it recreational suicide," she said. "We want to emphasize the client's willing participation in their own death as a therapeutic and life changing experience."

"Is it always beneficial?" he asked. Azreal thought of a kimono clad girl falling from the 13th floor a week ago. The parents hadn't seen their daughter fall, but they had been sitting too close in the lobby. No one had thought to keep them inside until it was too late.

Their aloof demeanors had crumbled at the sight of their daughter lying sprawled on the concrete. There hadn't been as much blood as one might expect, despite the gaping wound in the girl's stomach. The entire event felt cinematic to Azreal, as if what she saw was just fake blood and spirit gum... until the elevator doors opened.

Out had stepped the other daughter, the twin, with a look of elation glowing on her face. It had chilled Azreal to see that incriminating, obvious joy. She had started the Bitter Suites as a path to life appreciation. The 30 seconds it took the girl to step out of the elevator and walk to her parents had shaken Azreal's belief in herself. Maybe her father had been right about renewable death. She remembered Killian's question.

"So far it has always been beneficial… at least to someone," she answered. He raised his eyebrows at her, but she refused to elaborate. Instead, she turned her attention to his papers and realized she felt tired on a subatomic level.

She thumbed through the stack without reading. Everything looked in order and Azreal had lost five resuscitators in the aftermath of the recent fiasco. Appointments had been canceled, which raised questions. She didn't need questions. She needed resuscitators to fill teams. She needed business to continue as usual.

"When can you start?" she asked. "I can have you in orientation beginning tomorrow." Killian looked surprised, and then his face lit up in a boyish grin.

"This is my lucky day," he said. I was worried you wouldn't like me. How long is orientation?"

"Liking you has nothing to do with hiring you. You're qualified and I'm shorthanded. Orientation lasts a week, unless you don't pass your clearances." Azreal wondered if closing the Bitter Suites for a week would raise too many questions, and then dismissed the idea. If she couldn't keep things running smooth, she'd have a media nightmare on her hands. She rifled through papers under her desk and pulled one out.

"Here's the orientation details. I'll expect you tomorrow morning with your work cards." He leaned forward and took her hand and shook it. His touch was cool and strong.

"I'll be here, caffeinated and ready to go. You just got yourself a new resuscitator." Azreal smiled at him with gratitude and then she tightened her jaw until it vanished. Her exhaustion was making her too friendly.

"Okay, tomorrow then." Killian walked out of the lobby and entered the street. A few blocks away he entered a rundown apartment complex with painted windows and dirty halls. He climbed the stairway to the fifth floor and juggled his key in a warped door that seemed to be made of chipped layers of paint rather than wood.

Inside, a dark haired, tattooed girl lay on a double mattress beneath the scratched window. Feet on the wall, she was reading on her phone. She rolled over and sat up, tossing her phone to one side as he closed the door behind him.

"Well?" she asked.

"Yoshiko, darling, you look like you need a dose of life appreciation. I suggest you make yourself an appointment at the Bitter Suites." She jumped up and hugged him. They stood like that for a minute, grinning and embracing each other.

"When should I schedule my experience?" she asked. She held up one of her tattooed arms, covered in a rose and web pattern, and tapped the image of a widow spider on her forearm. "We've been waiting for over a year." He kissed the spider mark, and then her.

"I'll be ready in a week," he said. The girl retrieved her phone from the bed.

"I guess I better make myself an appointment then."

Piece of Cake

Azreal didn't look up when she first heard the lobby doors open and footsteps approach her desk. She knew it was her next appointment. When she did look up, she found herself once again surprised, and she couldn't place why.

The petite woman smiling at her wasn't remarkable. Probably late 20s with hair cut in a plain, black bob, the most distinctive thing about her was the network of spider webs and roses tattooed on her arms like sleeves. Body art wasn't unusual, especially for the clientele of the Bitter Suites. They tended to be the creative types.

"Can I help you?" asked Azreal, despite knowing why the girl was here.

"I have an appointment for a simple suicide," she answered. "Yoshiko Aki. I called last week."

"Of course," said Azreal. "I have your booking right here." She found the correct keycard and held it to herself rather than handing it over. "You decided to try a pretty straight forward suicide." The girl nodded.

"Yep, I finally decided to see what all the hubbub was about but I thought I'd go basic at first. Looking forward to it." Still, Azreal didn't hand over the keycard. There was something bothering her about this situation, and she needed to know what.

"So it is your first time dying?" she asked. The girl nodded again, glanced at the keycard and then looked back up at Azreal.

"Is that okay? Should I have done something to prepare?" The girl raised her eyebrows with her question. It was her attitude, Azreal decided. The usual clients were seeking something—fulfillment, closure, thrills—this girl wanted none of that. Her attitude was efficient and businesslike.

"I'm just always curious as to what brings people to the Bitter Suites," said Azreal. "The reasons to die are as interesting as the experience itself. What brings you here?"

The girl reached into a small purse and pulled out her phone. She poked the screen for a moment, navigating, and then held it up to Azreal. It was a list titled *Things I Want to Try Before I Die*. First on the list was 1. *Renewable death.*

That explains the all business attitude, thought Azreal. *This girl isn't here for the experience. She's here to check something off of a bucket list.* Out loud, she gave a little chuckle and slid the keycard across the desk.

"Thank you for sharing that," she said. "You didn't seem like my usual client. I just wondered." The girl picked up the keycard and shrugged.

"I've been accused of never being able to do anything without some kind of motive for achievement. I just wanted to show my family and friends that I could do things just for the experience." She slipped her phone back in her bag. "I don't mention the list, though. It just proves them right. The achievement I'm after now is to prove them wrong." That satisfied Azreal.

"Your secret is safe with me," she said. "I hope you get a good experience out of this." The girl flashed Azreal a bright smile—too bright—and a flash of keen triumph was evident. It bothered Azreal again and reminded her of a kitten, something friendly to everyone but the meal, then the look was gone. Azreal decided she was still too keyed up over recent events and seeing ghosts where there were none.

"Have a beautiful death," she said, dismissing her. There was nothing to worry about today. She had a full resuscitator crew on staff and a relatively simple day scheduled. She deserved a few minutes of peace. "Your experience waits for you on the second floor, room number is on your card." The girl thanked her and headed off to fulfill a check on a list. Azreal sincerely hoped she got more than just that.

In the elevator, Yoshiko let herself relax and the same predatory look Azreal had witnessed spread across her face, unchecked. She kissed the keycard, her eyes closed. The gesture was lingering, passionate and involved. No keycard at the Bitter Suites had ever received such a caress. Then the elevator dinged to announce her arrival.

Yoshiko glanced at the number on her card, and then at the directory on the wall before heading down the hall. She found her room door, slid her keycard and entered. In the shadow of the doorway, before she entered the room, she paused. She knew, for this moment, she had privacy.

She closed her eyes to keep the tears back. Inside, her nerves were quaking. She bit her lip and offered a silent prayer to anyone listening—God, her ancestors, luck and karma—before crossing herself. One hand slipped over her forearm to cover a widow spider tattooed there. Prayers done, she gathered her composure and entered the room.

A simple room, it was designed for budget deaths. A plain bed, a desk and chair, industrial carpet designed for durability… overseeing the sparse room was a wall sized mirror and a door.

Yoshiko glanced at the mirror and gave a half smile. It comforted her to know there was a resuscitator team, particularly one resuscitator, so close. She sensed him there, encouraging, and knew she was safe. She put her bag in the chair and pulled her phone out again. Navigating to her list, she checked it as done and held it up to her reflection in the glass.

"Crossed off my list, so no turning back," she said to the mirror. "I know you guys do this all the time. I'm just here to prove a point, so let's just get it done with quickly." She smiled at those that she knew listened. "I won't say I'm nervous, but please don't let me fall off a balcony."

She knew they were wincing behind the glass. The Bitter Suites couldn't afford another screw up like a few weeks ago. All the resuscitators would be hyper alert to make this, and every death, run smooth. She and Killian were counting on it.

She set her phone down on the chair next to her bag and looked at the small bottle on the dresser. She had picked poison because she knew it would be hard to do anything else. Her natural survival instinct was so strong she wouldn't be able to cut herself. She had tried before. Everyone had limitations.

She picked up the bottle and read the tag. *Drink me.* Popping the safety seal, she unscrewed the cap and held the tiny bottle up to the mirror like a toast before swallowing the contents. Yoshiko set the bottle down and lay down on the bed to wait. She closed her eyes, keeping her breath even.

She had never died before, and she was curious as to how it would feel. She noted the slowing of her breath and felt a sadness wash over her. She loved life, even at its worst. Saying goodbye, even for a few moments, was tough. The potential for not coming back was slim, but there.

Worse than permanent death was getting caught. That meant the end of life for both of them—at least anything that could be called life. They would be imprisoned, vital organs sold to pay their debt to society and spend the rest of their existence as vegetables hooked up to the grid, generating power until they expired or their sentence was fulfilled. No one ever came back after serving as a bio battery. They had put everything on this one grift. If they succeeded, they were set for life. If they failed... Yoshiko forced the thought away.

Everything was already in play and there was no turning back. The poison was in her system, slowing her thoughts and turning her eyelids to lead. A tear made its way from the corner of one eye to escape its dying host before dropping to the pillow to expire anyway. Her part in this was done. All she had to do now was let go. She did, one sluggish plea for luck limping through her thoughts before they stilled. She exhaled.

Behind the glass, Killian struggled to keep his emotions in check as he watched his partner die. He fiddled nervously with the ring on his finger, realized what he was doing and carefully moved his hands apart. So much was riding on this, he couldn't afford to let feelings taint him, but they welled up nonetheless. As she let go her final breath, he choked in his throat.

"Dude, relax," said the tech he was paired with, Ron. "You've been doing great all week. Nothing fancy with this one. Piece of cake. Azreal doesn't just hire anyone." Killian grinned at him, affecting a squeamish face. *Except this time*, thought Killian.

"I think I drank too much last night," he said. "Let's get her back up asap so

I can pop a painkiller." Ron nodded, grabbing his gear. Killian popped the door open and entered the room, followed by the other resuscitator.

"Alright, like clockwork," he said. "I'll shoot her up, you keep from getting freaked out by the needle." His co-worker's eyes bulged and he sucked in his breath with surprise.

"Seriously, that's not a joke. If Azreal found out I'd be gone." Ron lowered his voice even more and glanced at the girl on the bed. "There is no room here for resuscitators with trypanophobia. I'm in counseling for it. I can't believe I ever told you."

Killian could. As soon as he'd passed the orientation intake he'd looked for the weakest link in the group. Ron was it. Cast off on the edge of the herd, the stragglers were always easy marks. All it took was an invitation for a few beers after work and Ron had given them the final key to pull off this all off. Killian and Yoshiko needed someone who wouldn't watch them too closely. Ron couldn't watch needles. It was a match made… somewhere. Killian clapped him on the back.

"I'm not going to say anything. Don't look and you won't freak out. I got you covered. Just sit behind me so it looks like you're doing your job." Killian pulled the barcoded hypodermic out of his bag and unsheathed it. Predictably, Ron blanched, sat on the edge of the bed and turned away. Killian pulled the girl's arm out straight, eyes fixed on the widow's hourglass.

"Hey, check her vitals and make sure she's gone," he said. The meditech complied, feeling behind her knee without looking at Killian.

"No activity from the popliteal artery. She's gone. Just do it."

Killian still wasn't sure how closely they were being monitored so he was taking no chances. He slid his hand under his bag and fingered his ring. The black stone was connected by bluetooth to a tiny, spike mechanism they had implanted in her upper nasal cavity. A pretty girl who could nosebleed on command was a handy diversion.

"Alright, bringing her back up," he said. He pressed the stone and thought he heard the tiniest crunch from Yoshiko's face. On cue, the blood started running out of her left nostril. Without hesitation Killian moved the needle to the hourglass mark and injected the syringe contents into the silicone tube they had surgically implanted there. He pulled the needle out and reinserted it into the crook of her elbow.

"Shit! She's bleeding,' he said. Ron twisted around to get a look and Killian made sure Ron bumped him. He dropped the empty syringe on the bedspread and cursed.

"I think I missed the vein!" He turned to Ron. "Stop jumping around. You're shaking the whole bed!" He stood up and stepped back. "I did miss. Her bleeding should be done by now. Give me your backup." Ron fumbled in his own kit and pulled out the syringe that had been assigned to him.

"Fine, just hit her again. I'll say mine leaked and take care of the paperwork." He handed the syringe full of nanomeds to Killian with a shaking hand. Taking it, Killian repositioned the needle and pushed the plunger in. He could barely breath from excitement. Everything was going perfect.

"Nanomeds successful. Time!" Ron checked the timer hanging at his waist. His lips moved silently as he counted down. The blood stopped streaming out of Yoshiko's nose and they held their breath. The man timing held up three fingers and started a countdown.

"One," said Ron in a low voice. "Our girl should be back up." Neither of them moved. They watched her face for any signs of life. Yoshiko lay still, her features frozen into a waxy expression of slumber she wasn't coming out of.

There always has to be a glitch, Killian thought. *She's not going to come back.* Killian felt his heart slide down the inside of his ribs as it shriveled, and then Yoshiko inhaled with a spasm. Ron exhaled in relief. Killian blinked back tears.

"Holy crap, that felt close," he said. Ron elbowed him, shook his head and motioned towards the girl who was coming back to consciousness. He was pale and trembling. Killian shrugged, gave a goofy expression and mouthed the word *oops* back.

"Piece of cake," he said out loud. Yoshiko's eyes fluttered open, fell on Killian and she gave a weak smile.

"Thanks for bringing me back... guys," she said in a small voice. "But I probably won't be one of your regular customers." She grimaced and swallowed with an ill expression.

"Your stomach is still processing the poison," said Killian. He twisted the top off of a tube of milky liquid from his bag and handed it to her. "This will help." She drank it and closed her eyes. "We'll run some brief health scans on you, to make sure you are recovered, and let you get some rest. I just want to look inside your nose, first, if you don't mind."

Killian bent forward, aiming a light into her bloody nostrils. He made a show of conducting a thorough search, even swabbing her nasal cavities. He avoided the pin modification he knew was implanted in her nasal mucosa. After a few minutes of intensive study, he wiped her face clean, sat back and switched the light off.

"Looks good in there," he said. "You may want to up your liquid intake. Dehydration and stress probably caused your nose bleed. You look healthy." He glanced at the other tech and noted the look of relief spreading across his face. "Take a break. I'll take her vitals and clear her." Ron nodded and sat down in a chair with an audible exhale.

Killian ran a scanner over Yoshiko's body, covering nearly every inch, looking for abnormalities. He passed around the spider tattooed on her forearm, knowing it would trip the sensor alarm, and sat back again.

"You are back to full health and good to go when you feel up to it," he said. "Please be aware that the nanomeds will stay active in your system for a length of 30 days. During that time you will find yourself enjoying extraordinary health and a resistance to damage. If you should become catastrophically damaged during the 30 day period while the nanomeds are active, your body will be repaired back to its original state. If you have any other ailments due to disease and former injury, the nanomeds will repair you. Please remember that after the 30 day period expires, so do the nanomeds. You will no longer be invincible, so take advantage and enjoy, but don't take them for granted." She pushed herself upright.

"Noted," she said. "I don't want to be unappreciative, but do you think I could get out of here? I'm sorry, but I'm over the whole death experience." She gave a tired smile to both of them. Together, the techs started gathering their things.

"You bet," said Killian. "I hope you enjoyed your experience with us and will come back." She shrugged. Ron bagged the empty syringes for the logs.

"Maybe. Right now I can't plan farther than dinner. How can people enjoy that?" The two meditechs finished gathering equipment and backed out of the room, closing the door.

Alone, Yoshiko slid off the bed and gathered her bag up. She smoothed her hair in the mirror and carefully dabbed her nose with a tissue before walking out of the room. She wore exhaustion on her face like a mask.

In contrast to her outward appearance, her heart tripped inside of her ribs, hammering with a panicked beat. She kept her steps even and measured. They were so close to pulling off the scam they had been waiting a year to execute. Down the elevator, the doors slid open to reveal the desk attendant busy shuffling papers while on the phone.

"Yes, sir, I do have an opening for this week. What kind of death were you looking for?" Azreal looked up, saw her and gave a small wave, motioning her over. Yoshiko's feet wanted to refuse the beckon and pound their way to the door and freedom, but she kept them obedient and approached.

Still on the phone, Azreal slid a small book of coupons across the desk to her. *Thank you for choosing the Bitter Suites,* Azreal mouthed to her. Yoshiko wanted to giggle with relief but she held herself in check. Nodding with a polite smile, she pocketed the booklet and walked to the door with calm, even steps. The door slid open, and Yoshiko passed through, leaving the Bitter Suites.

She didn't allow herself to relax, no triumphant smiles, until she entered the seedy, one room flat she had shared with Killian the past year. Once she had locked the door, she allowed herself a tiny whoop of joy and she held her spider tattoo, and it's hidden treasure, to her chest.

Killian would be returning soon to share the celebration. They would have wine and then he would cut into her arm, removing the silicon micro barrel that had been implanted there. For a year it had waited for this day. She could feel the unfamiliar weight under her skin, subtle as it was, and knew that it ensured their future.

"Why I did enjoy my stay at the Bitter Suites," Yoshiko replied to a faraway Azreal, at that moment drafting a press release about the hotel's new safety guidelines. "And I think I got everything I needed from it."

She lay back on the bed, smiling large, to wait for Killian to come home.

Popover

Azreal gave me a scowl as soon as I walked through the door.

"Hang on," I said. "Before you go judging me, you need to listen."

Azreal slammed her books closed. I'd never seen her so angry before.

"I don't need to listen. I *own* the Bitter Suites. I *created* the Bitter Suites. *I make the rules.*" Even angry she was pretty, but I wasn't here to flirt. I'd tried to go down that road long ago and decided Azreal just wasn't human.

"Seriously, you made me this way." I put on my sweetest face and puckered my lips to evoke her sympathy, if she had any. "Please, Azreal. I got nothing left but this."

"You are a junkie. It hasn't even been 30 days. I should have never let you through the doors." She picked up the phone receiver and mashed a button with vengeance. Her eyes didn't look so pretty when they were narrowed on me like they were. "Killian, I need help in the lobby," she said. She slammed the phone back in the cradle. Now it was my turn to be angry.

I slid my hand along the counter knocking everything to the floor. A vase, business cards, brochures—all of it shattered and scattered across the polished marble of the lobby. Azreal flared her nostrils, turned crimson and slammed both hands down on the desk.

"I have enough to worry about right now without you coming in here… unwelcome…against the rules…" A man came through a door behind her and stopped, surveying the scene. He wasn't huge, but he had the determined, unafraid look of a bouncer. He started around the desk toward me.

I thought something like this might happen, so I'd taken precautions. Azreal had turned into a bitch lately with the death scene. Every time I come here lately there are more rules. I swear she's making them up just to keep me from living. I pulled the razor from my pocket and flipped it open.

"You're pushing me to do this, Azreal. I don't want to go this far, but you're making me. I have double the money!" The bouncer stopped and took a wary stance, gauging me I suppose. He needed to see how fast I was, how much of a danger. Azreal looked less angry.

"You need help," she said. "Let Killian help you." I shook my head and positioned the razor on my forearm, prepared to cut just like I'd been taught here my first visit—length wise and not cross wise, as instructed.

"I need this, Az. I *need* it," I said. Dammit, I could feel tears coming, the sting spreading up my cheeks and behind my eyeballs. I didn't want to blubber, but if it helped soften her up, fine. "Please don't send me away. You know I'll do it." Azreal's face turned stone.

"I still can't help you," she said. "The rules are in place to protect you. You don't even know what damage you are causing right now." This was no good. I was going to have to take my chances. Even if she didn't renege on her precious rules and dose me, I'd rather go out than continue to exist like this. I was like a moth in the dark, flitting from lamp to light, only existing in the burn. One way or another, I needed out. I dug the razor in and sliced deep.

Azreal made a small sob and clapped her hand over her mouth. Her eyes got all luminous with tears. I could see her struggling to compose herself and then she went all stony again. Meanwhile, I'm bleeding all over myself in the lobby.

"Killian, can you please escort this former client of the Bitter Suites off the property and inform him that, should he survive, he is banned from ever returning here. I will have the legals put in the paperwork." The guy walked over without missing a beat, hefted me up under my armpits and started pushing me towards the door.

"I'm not going anywhere," I yelled back. "I'm going to die on your doorstep and see how the press likes that!"

"Make sure he leaves our property if he is going to die," said Azreal as the guy shoved the glass door open and propelled me outside. I struggled against the guy but it was useless. It's not that he was stronger than me, I had let myself go the past year or so, but he kind of grabbed the back of my neck and coat and was moving me almost like a puppet. He had one of his arms twisted under mine in a weird kung fu lock. He almost broke my cut arm off shoving me through the door.

"Seriously, get off," I said, trying to free myself. He half pulled, half pushed me down the street and around the corner. I was leaving a trail of blood but no one bothered about that. I had the smug satisfaction that someone was going to have to clean it up when it started raining. The bouncer shoved me into a space between two dumpsters, dropped me and pulled out his phone.

"If you can pay double, I might be able to help you," he said to me. I nodded and reached into my jacket to pull out my wallet. I had cashed in everything I owned, and then everything my mom owned, to get this. I shoved it at him. I was getting weaker, but my spirits were the brightest they'd been all day. He took the wallet, opened it and counted out the cash.He pocketed my money and tossed the wallet back to me, turning around to make a call. I heard someone pick up on the line.

"I got our first customer," he said to the phone. "Can you meet me down here within 10 minutes? He's already half gone." He listened for the answer and replied. "Yea, bring a needle. He paid more than double but you gotta hurry. He's in the alley next to the BS. I have to get back." He slipped the phone back in his pocket.

"I gotta go, but a little half Asian chick is going to come help you. We got our own blend of nanos, and you're our first customer," he said. I kind of thought maybe he was just ripping me off, but what was I going to do about it? I was sitting in a puddle with a mix of garbage juice and my own blood soaking my trousers and I was feeling pretty weak. I'd gambled that sweet Azreal wouldn't be able to let me die. I'd been wrong, but maybe I'd found something better. This guy certainly wasn't spouting off about rules. He squatted down and got close to my face, his eyes drilling into me.

"This is between us, got it?" I think I nodded. "I can hook you up if you can keep the money coming but if you ever come back into the BS and mention me, I will kill you. There will be no coming back then. Got it?" My head was spinning and I was feeling kind of dumb.

"The BS? What's that?" Don't laugh, I was almost passing out by now from blood loss. Plus I think I'd forgotten to eat anything that day. He growled at me, grabbed my jacket lapel and kind of shook me.

"The Bitter Suites, asshole. Don't come back." Then he was gone. I heard him crunch his way down the alley. The drizzle was collecting on everything and water was running into my eyes and stinging them. I wasn't crying.

"I won't come back... cuz I'll be dead," I said to no one. "Probably." I slumped, resigned to the fact that no little half Asian chick was coming to save me. Azreal was never letting me back in the Bitter Suites. I had no friends left and I didn't even want to think about my mom. And I was thinking I'd just been robbed. I tried to turn over but I was stuck halfway in a smashed box. The words Hillsbro Cheddar Popovers was printed in orange along the side. *What the hell is a popover*, I wondered.

I heard footsteps crunching down the alley toward me and I thought maybe Killian was coming back to finish the job. They walked slowly and then stopped at me. I looked up and swear I saw an angel under a giant, red umbrella. It was a little half Asian chick for sure, with a cute bobbed haircut and a black raincoat. She had these tiny little red, rubber boots that looked like they were for toys. She kneeled down, propping the umbrella over us both between the dumpsters. She smiled at me, pulled out a syringe and my heart kind of collapsed inside me. Azreal had nothing on this goddess.

"I love you," I think I said. She pulled my arm out straight, found my vein and pumped me full of life saving, nano goodness. I think I told her I loved her again, or I was just blubbering, but can you blame me? I'd almost died, I mean for permanent. She held up a cheap phone in a clear bag. My eyes were all blurry but I could see what it was. I think I nodded.

"Next time you need a fix, call me," she said. "I'll fix you up. No wait time either." I know I was blubbering then. This day had gotten to the bottom most layer of shitty and then suddenly this girl was saving me, not just now, but for always.

"Screw the BS," I think I said. It must of been close because she smiled at me, made the *call me* signal with her hand and walked away, her big, red umbrella vanishing around the dumpster. There I lay in the rain, soaking in alley filth, waiting for the nanomeds to kick in. Already the bleeding had stopped and I was feeling better. Anyone who walked by might have mistook me for someone on the down-and-out, but who cares. It may have looked like I was lying in the rain between two dumpsters in an alley, but I knew the truth.

I was on top of the world.

Thanks for the R&R

If you enjoyed this book, please consider leaving a review. Every share shows you care!

About the Author

Angela Yuriko Smith is a two-time Bram Stoker Award–winning author, former president of the Horror Writers Association, and publisher of *Space and Time*. As a publishing consultant and coach, she helps writers build sustainable creative careers rooted in art, not arson. She writes *Authortunities* on Substack.

You can connect with me on:

https://angelaysmith.com

Subscribe to my newsletter:

https://authortunities.substack.com

Also by Angela Yuriko Smith

Angela Yuriko Smith is a third-generation Shimanchu/Ryukyuan-American, award-winning poet, author, and publisher with 20+ years of newspaper experience. Publisher of *Space & Time* magazine (est. 1966), two-time Bram Stoker Awards® Winner, and an HWA Mentor of the Year, she shares *Authortunities*, a free weekly calendar of author opportunities at authortunities.substack.com.

Inujini
With foreword by best-selling author Alma Katsu

Three indigenous Ryukyuan girls are stripped of everything in a war their people will gain nothing from, except loss. As they struggle to survive, they learn the power of resilience lies in connecting with who they were, who they are and who they will be together.

Kaori, Yuki and Shigeko are three island girls on the edge of womanhood who find themselves trapped in a fictionalized Battle of Okinawa. Based on true events, the three girls endure hunger, injury, humiliation and gender based violence as everything they love is stripped from them.

They each survive parallel story arcs that entwine in the last act as they connect to their intuition, in the form of the shiisaa guardians specific to Okinawa, and each other. Shamanistic magic may be what brings them together, but in the end it's the girls themselves that wind up being the heroines. Their sisterhood is what defies and defeats those that threaten them.

Trigger warning: Sexual violence is an essential part of the plot to represent the real life situation women in Okinawa face to this day, but there are no graphic depictions of the act in this story. It remains only a threat to the characters.

www.ingramcontent.com/pod-product-compliance
Lightning Source LLC
LaVergne TN
LVHW020657100826
845148LV00012B/2542
* 9 7 9 8 9 0 2 2 8 9 2 6 5 *